Sweet Valley

HIGH®

Secrets

Sweet Valley
HIGH ®

Double Love
Secrets

Sweet Valley HIGH.

Secrets

WRITTEN BY KATE WILLIAM

CREATED BY

FRANCINE PASCAL

LAUREL-LEAF BOOKS

Published by Laurel-Leaf
an imprint of Random House Children's Books
a division of Random House, Inc.
New York

Originally produced by Cloverdale Press
Originally published by Bantam Books, New York, in 1983.

Laurel-Leaf and colophon are registered trademarks of
Random House, Inc.
Sweet Valley High is a registered trademark of Francine Pascal.
Conceived by Francine Pascal.

Visit us on the Web! www.randomhouse.com/teens

Educators and librarians, for a variety of teaching tools, visit us at
www.randomhouse.com/teachers

Library of Congress Cataloging-in-Publication Data

William, Kate.
Secrets / written by Kate William ; created by Francine Pascal. — 1st Laurel-
Leaf ed.
p. cm. — (Sweet Valley High)
Summary: Beautiful and ruthless Jessica uses gossip to sabotage Enid, her
rival in the contest for queen of the fall dance at Sweet Valley High and
the best friend of her twin sister Elizabeth.
ISBN 978-0-440-42263-1 (pbk.)
[1. Twins—Fiction. 2. Contests—Fiction. 3. High schools—Fiction.
4. Schools—Fiction.] I. Pascal, Francine. II. Title.
PZ7.W65549Sf 2008
[Fic]—dc22
2007021041

RL: 6
April 2008
Printed in the United States of America
10 9 8 7 6 5 4 3 2 1
First Laurel-Leaf Edition

CHAPTER

/

JESSICA WAKEFIELD SMOOTHED the front of her new Hawaiian-print Roxy dress and held her head high as she strode along the outdoor walkway to her locker at Sweet Valley High. She heard a couple of giggles as she passed by a group of sophomores, but couldn't tell exactly whom they'd come from, so she just shot the whole group a look of death until they all clammed up; then she kept right on walking.

Sooner or later the chatter about what had happened to her last Saturday night was going to die down, and if Jessica had anything to say about it, it would be sooner rather than later.

Her best friends, Cara Walker and Lila Fowler, stood near the wall up ahead, their heads bent together as they chatted happily. Friendly faces. Thank God.

"Hey, guys!" Jessica called out, grabbing her lock.

Cara instantly closed her cell phone and shoved it behind her back, looking guilty.

"What was that?" Jessica asked suspiciously.

"Oh, nothing," Cara said. She turned to her own locker mirror to check her long, dark hair. Then she glanced sidelong at Lila and they both cracked up.

"You haven't deleted the pictures yet, have you," Jessica accused Cara, whipping open her locker. "Cara! You promised me you'd get rid of them!"

"We're sorry, Jess, but come on," Lila said, taking Cara's phone out of her hand. "These are hilarious."

She held out the phone with her perfectly manicured fingers, as if Jessica really wanted to see how Cara had caught the worst moment of her life on her camera phone. She glanced over, thinking maybe it hadn't been as bad as she recalled, and there she was, pulling herself out of the Sweet Valley High School pool, fully clothed, with black mascara running down her face. In the background, a couple of kids laughed as if they were about to bust something. Nope. It was just as bad as she remembered.

"I swear, if that little stunt Elizabeth pulled keeps me

2

from getting nominated for homecoming queen, I am going to take pictures of her in the shower and post them on her precious little blog," Jessica ranted, shoving a couple of books into her locker and closing it with a bang.

"God, Jess. Take a joke," Lila said, rolling her big brown eyes. She fished in her Louis Vuitton backpack for a pot of lip gloss and nudged Cara aside so that she could see her reflection while she applied. "Besides, half the school still thinks it was Liz who got dunked, not you. There's no way you don't make homecoming court."

Jessica sighed and looked in her locker mirror. Her shoulder-length blond hair looked perfect, not a strand out of place, and her new blue eyeliner really brought out her stunning Pacific blue eyes. The gold lavaliere necklace she always wore—a present from her parents on her sixteenth birthday—fell just above the neckline of her new dress. She looked perfect today, she knew. But homecoming court votes were already in. Looking perfect *today* wouldn't help her.

"You know, technically, we should still dump Liz in the pool," Cara pointed out, her green eyes thoughtful. "The tradition is that the Insider columnist gets dunked, right? Well, *Liz* is the Insider columnist, but she made us all believe you were her so that you would get dunked. Ergo, she needs to get wet."

Jessica smirked. "I like the way you think, Cara Walker."

"Since when do you say 'ergo'?" Lila asked, a tiny wrinkle in her otherwise beautiful tan brow.

"Since I started taking that SAT course," Cara responded with a sniff.

"Attention, students!" Principal Cooper's voice suddenly boomed over the PA system. "We have your results for this year's homecoming court."

"Omigod! This is it!" Jessica gasped, grabbing Lila's and Cara's arms. A sizzle of anticipation raced through the warm California air. Most of the people in the outdoor hallway stopped gabbing so they could hear. Jessica held her breath.

"First, your candidates for homecoming king," the principal announced. There was a shuffling of papers and he cleared his throat. "They are . . . Winston Egbert."

"What?" Jessica cried, causing Lila and Cara to laugh. "Is this the joke court?" Winston was basically the biggest dork in school. Jessica had always thought he looked just like that Waldo guy from the *Where's Waldo?* books.

"Ken Matthews," the principal continued.

"Okay, well at least *that* makes sense," Jessica added as Ken, the gorgeous, blond captain of the football team, accepted congratulations from his friends down the hall.

"Bruce Patman."

Yes! Jessica cheered silently. She'd had a crush on Bruce ever since she'd known what the word "crush" meant, and she'd been counting on his making the homecoming court.

"And Todd Wilkins," the principal finished.

"Shocker," Lila said, rolling her eyes.

Of course Elizabeth's perfect boyfriend would make it. If he didn't, he might be less than perfect.

"And now your candidates for homecoming queen," Principal Cooper continued. "Lila Fowler."

Lila preened, flicking her light brown hair over her shoulder and running a fingertip along one plucked eyebrow. The people around her applauded, and Jessica smiled, even though inside she was burning with jealousy and dread. Jealousy that Lila always got everything, dread that her own name might not also be on the list.

"Enid Rollins."

"Okay. Now I *know* this is a joke," Jessica said.

"Hey!" Lila protested, whacking her with the back of her hand.

"What? I mean, Enid? Come on. She might be an even bigger loser than Winston," Jessica said.

"And she's your sister's best friend," Lila pointed out. "So what does that make Liz?"

Jessica shot Lila a silencing look. Jessica could bad-mouth

her twin as much as she wanted, but she didn't like it when other people tried to do the same.

"You get one hot boyfriend and all of a sudden you're homecoming court material," Cara said with a sigh, leaning back against the wall.

"You think that's why? Because she's going out with Ronnie Edwards?" Jessica asked, incredulous.

"Well, he's new. He's hot. He's all mysterious and brooding," Cara said with a shrug. "When she snagged him it totally upped her It factor."

Jessica pondered this. She'd never quite thought of Ronnie Edwards as mysterious and brooding—more silent and robotic—but she could see how some girls might find him attractive. Maybe Cara was on to something.

"Elizabeth Wakefield," the principal continued.

Oh, please, please, please let the last name be mine! Jessica begged the popularity gods.

"And Jessica Wakefield," he finished.

"Yes!" Jessica shouted, jumping up and down.

Cara laughed, but Lila shot her a look of disdain. "Very sophisticated, Jess. Not at all embarrassing."

Jessica composed herself and accepted congratulations from Ken and his friends as they passed by. Then she saw Bruce himself come around the corner, and it was as if everything just switched into slow motion. He walked down the center of the hall as though he owned the place, his dark hair shiny in the sun, that perpetual smirk in his brown eyes. He was wearing a pristine blue Ralph Lauren sweater and distressed jeans, and looked like he could sail off on his yacht at any second. Which, of course, with his family's money, he could probably do. Jessica watched him until he strolled by, hoping for that rare and coveted hello.

"Ladies," he said with a brief nod.

Jessica almost melted.

"Wow, Jess. You look like you just saw your first Roberto Cavalli," Lila commented snidely. "Try rolling your tongue back into your mouth."

Cara snorted a laugh that brought Jessica back to earth.

"I don't care what you think, Lila," Jessica said, tossing her hair back. She gave herself a confident, steadying look in the mirror, hoping her crazy heartbeat would chill out before she overheated. "Bruce Patman is going to be mine eventually. And now that we're in homecoming court together, I'm that much closer."

● ● ●

"Liz. We need to talk," Enid Rollins announced from the doorway of her best friend's bedroom that night.

7

Elizabeth Wakefield looked up from her computer, her blue-green eyes amused. "Oh God. Are you breaking up with me?" she joked.

"Liz! I'm totally serious!" Enid wailed, striding into the room. She was wearing a black Juicy Couture sweat suit and had tied her long, wavy brown hair up in a high ponytail. She'd been hoping to make herself feel better by slipping on her comfy clothes, but her heart still felt as if it were tied in knots. She dropped her overnight bag and pillow on Elizabeth's vintage settee and plopped down next to them, head in her hands. Her ponytail fell forward, hiding her face. "I don't know what to do. You have to tell me what to do."

Her pulse was pounding a mile a minute. On her way over to the Wakefields', Enid had tried to psych herself up to tell Elizabeth everything—all the secrets she'd been keeping bottled up for so long. She'd even had a whole speech planned. But now that she was here and Liz was looking at her all concerned, she'd forgotten just about everything.

"Okay, now you're scaring me," Elizabeth said, rolling her chair around the desk so she was facing Enid, just inches away. She pushed up the sleeves of her soft pink sweater and leaned forward. "What's the matter?"

Enid took a deep breath and looked up. "It's Ronnie," she said. "I think he's going to break up with me."

Elizabeth's jaw dropped. "Why?"

"Because!" Enid said, standing and pacing over to the window. "Because he's going to find out what I did, and as soon as he finds that out he's going to think I'm a total psycho loser."

Elizabeth laughed and sat back in her chair. "You're not a psycho loser," she said kindly. "And what did you do that was so horrifying?"

Enid looked over her shoulder at Liz, biting her lip. She toyed with the window lock, snapping it back and forth, back and forth. She couldn't believe she was about to do this. She was actually going to confide in someone other than her parents, who naturally knew all. But she needed advice. And who could she trust more than her best friend?

"You have to promise me you won't hate me if I tell you," she said.

"Enid. Come on. How bad could it be?" Elizabeth asked, still not quite grasping the gravity of the situation.

"It's bad. You have to promise," Enid said firmly.

Elizabeth stood up, crossing her arms over her chest. "All right, then. I promise."

Taking a deep breath, Enid turned away from the window. She wiped her sweaty palms on her pants and braced herself. "I was arrested."

Elizabeth gasped. "What? When? For what?"

"It was about two years ago," Enid said, pacing over to the bed. "My parents were getting divorced and I was kind of freaking out. I started hanging out with these kids I'd known from camp who went to another school. A total druggie crowd, you know?" She glanced at Elizabeth to see how she was taking all this. Liz listened intently. "Anyway, there was this one guy, Geo. His name's actually George—George Warren—but he had everyone call him Geo. We kind of started hooking up and stuff, and he was into all this crap. Drinking and . . . other stuff." Enid stopped and swallowed hard, covering her face with her hands. "God, I don't even want to look at you right now."

"Enid. It's okay. It's fine," Elizabeth said, going over to sit on the bed. She grabbed Enid's wrist and pulled her down gently to sit next to her. "What happened?"

Enid sniffled and slid one of Liz's eyelet throw pillows onto her lap, toying with the lace edge. "One night things got a little out of hand. We mixed all this stuff. Totally stupid. We took E and drank an entire bottle of vodka out of his parents' bar and smoked a little. I was a complete mess, but Geo was even worse. Then we decided we were both starving and we just *had* to go out and get burgers . . . and I didn't have my license yet, so Geo drove."

"Oh God," Elizabeth said under her breath.

"Yeah. Not good," Enid added. "We got into an acci-dent. This little kid . . . he just came running into the street out of nowhere, and Geo wasn't even looking. . . ."

Tears spilled over onto Enid's cheeks. That moment was burned in her brain with more clarity than any other moment she had lived through so far. The squeal of the tires. The screams of the boy's mother. The song that had been playing on the radio. Her own voice coming from somewhere outside herself, just repeating over and over, "I'm so sorry. I'm so sorry. . . ."

"What happened to him?" Elizabeth asked quietly.

"He lived, but he was paralyzed from the waist down," Enid said, reaching for a tissue. "Permanently."

"Oh my God," Elizabeth said, covering her mouth with her hand.

"I know." Enid looked at the pillow in her lap morosely. "I know. It's awful. I still don't believe it sometimes."

"So . . . then what? Did you have a trial or some-thing?" Elizabeth asked.

"No. There was a plea bargain and we were both put on probation. We had to go to drug counseling and do community service. Geo's parents have money, so they settled out of court to basically take care of the kid—the victim—for life, which was good, I guess," Enid rambled.

"But after that I realized what a mess I was. I got the help I needed and eventually transferred into SVH, but Geo's parents sent him to boarding school. Which is what brings me to my current problem."

Enid paused. Her nose was clogged and she was totally overwhelmed by the amount of information she'd just spewed. It was the first time she'd ever told anyone the whole truth, and she was petrified to look at Elizabeth. Then, out of nowhere, Liz hugged her.

"I'm so sorry you had to go through all that," Liz said, squeezing Enid tightly.

Enid closed her eyes, pressing out a few fresh tears—these happy and relieved—and clung to her friend. She should have known that Elizabeth wouldn't look at her any differently. Liz was not only a good friend, but also a good person. Enid had always known that.

"So what do you mean, your current problem?" Elizabeth asked, leaning back again. She plucked a few more tissues from the box and handed them to Enid.

"Well—" Enid blew her nose hard and sniffled. "Geo—George—is coming back to town in a couple of weeks, and he wants to see me."

"But you don't want to see him," Elizabeth ventured.

"No! I'd love to see him. We still keep in touch on e-mail and stuff. We're friends," Enid explained. "It was really hard for him after everything that happened, and I was the only person who was really there for him."

Elizabeth's brow furrowed. "Okay. So I don't get the problem."

"The problem is Ronnie!" Enid blurted out. "We've only been going out for a few weeks. If some random guy shows up and wants to spend time with me, he's going to want to know why. What am I going to tell him?"

Elizabeth shrugged. "Tell him the truth."

A shiver shot right through Enid's heart at the very thought, and she pushed herself off the bed, hugging herself.

"No. No way."

"Enid, I know it's hard, but you told me. And it's not like there's a Liz-shaped hole in the wall over there," Liz joked, pointing over her shoulder. "I'm still here. What you did is in the past. You're an amazing person. I think you're even *more* amazing now that I know what you've had to deal with."

Enid smiled. "Really?"

"Totally," Liz said. "If it were me, I'd tell Todd."

"Yeah, but Todd's not the jealous type, Liz. Ronnie is." Enid gulped down a lump in her throat. "Forget the arrest and all that. He'd freak if he even knew I've been writing to some guy and didn't tell him."

Elizabeth shifted on the bed, fully facing Enid, her hands pressed into the bedspread. "But if you explained it just the way you did to me—"

"There's no way." Enid shook her head. "Remember last week when he saw me talking to John Pfeiffer before class? He completely freaked. And that was just going over homework."

Elizabeth stood up and walked over to her desk, clearly pondering the problem. "Okay, so no one knows about the e-mails but you and me, right?" she said.

"Nope." Enid shook her head.

"So the problem is that George wants to see you and you don't know what you'd tell Ronnie?" Elizabeth prompted.

"Right."

"Well, as I see it, you have two options. You either see George and you don't tell Ronnie about it, or you don't see George," Elizabeth said matter-of-factly. "Which is probably a better idea, because if anyone saw you with him it would totally get back to Ronnie. You know how the SVH rumor mill works. Just tell him you don't think it would be fair to your boyfriend to see him or something like that."

Enid felt all the color draining from her face. "Okay, there's just one tiny problem with that plan."

"What?" Elizabeth asked.

Enid winced. "I kind of already told George I was dying to see him."

• • •

"I have a special folder for all my e-mails with George," Enid said.

Elizabeth sat back in her desk chair as her friend brought up her e-mail account to show Liz her last response to George. Enid's fingers trembled over the keyboard, and Liz's heart went out to her. It had to have been insanely difficult for Enid to confess everything she'd just confessed. Liz just hoped that getting it off her chest would eventually make her feel somewhat better.

"Darn. It won't open," Enid said, double-clicking the folder.

"That keeps happening. I need to defrag this thing," Liz said, reaching for the mouse. "Here. I'll just drag the folder to the desktop. That usually works for some reason."

Elizabeth deposited the folder marked "George" on the desktop; then Enid reclaimed the mouse and opened two different messages.

"Okay. There they are. George's last e-mail and my reply," Enid said, stepping back from the desk.

"Okay, let's see. Maybe you weren't totally encouraging.

Maybe you still have wiggle room to get out of it." She leaned forward in her chair to read.

Hey Enid,

God, exams suck. I know they want to prepare us for college, but this is out of control. I had three two-hour tests yesterday alone. And these are just midterms. Finals will probably turn my head to complete mush. But I guess it's better if it turns to mush from studying than from anything else. ☺

Anyway, I just wanted to say thanks for your last e-mail. It was exactly the pep talk I needed to get me through the last few days. I'm actually coming home for fall break in a couple of weeks. Do you want to get together? I understand if you think it would be weird, but it would be cool if we could. Whatever. Just . . . let me know. I hope you're doing well, Enid.

Love,

George

P.S. Say hi to Winston for me.

"Wow," Elizabeth said.

"What?" Enid asked. "Oh, the Winston thing? Yeah, he was at camp with us, so George knows him."

"No. Not the Winston thing. This guy really likes you," Liz told her.

"What? No, he doesn't. I told you. We're just friends," Enid said.

"Oh, please. Look how he's trying to be so casual about wanting to see you! He's trying to throw you off," Elizabeth said. "He's totally crushing."

"Okay, shut up. You don't know what you're talking about. Look at my response already," Enid said, blushing. Elizabeth smirked but did as she was told.

> George,
> It wouldn't be weird at all. I would love to see you. You have my cell number. Just call when you get into town. Yay!
> —Enid

"Yeah. No wiggle room there," Liz said wryly. "If you don't see him after sending that message, you'll break his heart."

Enid groaned. "There's no way I can get out of it?"

"Enid, listen. Whatever feelings George may be having for you aside, maybe you're overreacting about Ronnie," Elizabeth said, minimizing the window. "Maybe he'd be . . . I don't know . . . glad to hear how loyal you are to your friends."

"He wouldn't see it that way," Enid said stubbornly. "I have to do whatever I can to keep him from finding out. I love him so much, Liz. I don't want to hurt him."

"I know. But what are you going to do?" Elizabeth asked her friend.

"I don't know. I'll think of something," Enid said. "But you have to promise me you won't tell anyone about this until I figure it out, okay? Not about the arrest. Not about the e-mails. Nothing."

"I promise I won't say a thing," Elizabeth told her, growing serious.

If there was one thing Elizabeth could understand, it was Enid's fear of having her secrets get out. Sweet Valley High was not a fun place to be when a girl became the center of a scandal. Liz had found that out firsthand just a couple of weeks back, when her eternally two-faced twin sister was brought home by the police but led them to believe that she was Elizabeth. After that, Elizabeth had found out who her real friends were, and it hadn't been pretty. Enid was one of the few who had stuck by her.

"Thanks, Liz," Enid said, reaching over for a hug. "You're pretty much the best friend ever."

"Ditto," Elizabeth replied.

They pulled back and Elizabeth rolled her eyes. "All

right. Enough with the mushy stuff. Let's go watch a movie!" She put her computer on standby and headed for the hall.

"Oh God. What did you rent? Please tell me it's not another stalker-slasher-horror thing," Enid wailed, grabbing her pillow and trailing after Liz. "The last one you picked gave me nightmares."

"I *promise* it's not a stalker-slasher-horror thing," Elizabeth said over her shoulder, her blue-green eyes sparkling. "Only two out of the three."

"Liz!" Enid protested with a laugh.

Elizabeth jogged down the stairs, shrieking as Enid chased her with her pillow. At least she had managed to lighten her best friend's mood, for now. Elizabeth just hoped that nothing would come of this whole Ronnie-George-Enid triangle and the history behind it. Because if she knew anything about the kids at SVH, it was that they would *love* to get hold of a scandal like this one.

CHAPTER
2

JESSICA STARED OUT the window at the sloping green lawns of Sweet Valley High as Ms. Dalton, her young and annoyingly gorgeous French teacher, droned on about verb conjugation.

I bore, you bore . . . this is totally boring! Jessica thought. Outside, a warm California breeze rustled the palm trees. Jessica took a deep breath and sighed, imagining herself at the beach, lying on a towel in the sun, wearing her new white bikini. She lifted her head, tossing her blond hair back as Bruce Patman emerged from the waves, the sun glinting off his dripping-wet skin. He grinned and strode toward her, tan and ripped and perfect, looking at her as if she were the only girl in the world. . . .

"Jessica? We're waiting."

With a start, Jessica sat up straight. The first thing she saw was Winston Egbert gazing at her from across the aisle all goofy and lovesick. The sight of him and his thick glasses pretty much obliterated any thoughts of Bruce.

"Sorry, Ms. Dalton," Jessica said, grimacing quickly at Winston. "What was the question?"

Ms. Dalton's pretty hazel eyes sparkled. She walked toward Jessica's desk in her chic skirt and top, as slim and tall as a supermodel. Every pair of male eyes in the room followed her. Except, unfortunately, Winston's.

"I was just wondering if you might like to let us in on the secret," Ms. Dalton said with a smile.

"Secret?" Jessica echoed, squirming.

"*Oui.* The secret of how you expect to conjugate the verbs I've written on the board, if you're looking out the window," she said.

All the kids in the room chuckled, and Jessica's face burned. She glanced over at Lila, who paused in her nail filing to shoot Jessica an irritated look. *Who does this woman think she is?* Lila's eyes said.

"Mental telepathy!" Winston said, attempting to come to her rescue.

"Excuse me?" Ms. Dalton asked.

"Jessica's *on the list*. You know . . . like in *Heroes*? She has powers mere mortals like us could never understand," Winston rambled. "She can even run faster than a speeding bullet."

"That's Superman, dude," Ken Matthews said from the back of the classroom, where he sat with his long legs sprawled across the aisle. "You'd better watch it. They'll take away your geek squad card for making a mistake like that."

Everyone in the classroom laughed, and Jessica shot Ken a grateful smile. Like Winston, Ken had no problem speaking up in class without being called on. The difference was that Ken was tall, blond and Abercrombie hot, while Winston was . . . Winston.

"Thank you for your input, Ken," Ms. Dalton said dryly. "Now let's all settle down and get to work. Unless any of you has X-ray vision and can see the answers through my notebook."

Jessica laughed at her lame joke, kissing up along with a few other students. Ken, however, flashed Ms. Dalton an incredibly sexy smile. Jessica shook her head as she bent over her notebook. Could his crush on Dalton be any more obvious? Everyone in school knew that he spent their afternoon tutoring sessions fawning over the woman, but Jessica didn't need to see it, thank you very much. The very thought of hot-as-sin Ken flirting with ancient Dalton . . . the two of them giggling, making eewy-gooey eyes at each other . . . ugh! Sometimes Jessica seriously detested her vivid imagination.

Don't think about it. Think about Bruce. . . .

And there he was, dressed in an impeccable blue suit, gliding up to her house in his black Cadillac XLR Roadster with the top down, his ice blue eyes smiling as he picked her up for the dance. . . .

Of course, he'd have to ask her first. Unless she decided to ask him. Which just made her insides squirm like a bucketful of worms. She shifted in her seat, irritated, and changed the scene in her mind.

Now she was at the dance with a nameless, faceless guy on her arm. Ronnie Edwards, who was a member of the homecoming committee, stood onstage, holding a small white card.

"Your homecoming king is . . . Bruce Patman!" he read.

Of course Bruce would win. He was the most popular, coveted, feared guy in school. Everyone would vote for him.

In her mind's eye, Bruce sauntered up to the stage and accepted his crown. Then Ronnie looked down at his card again.

"And your homecoming queen is . . . of course . . . Jessica Wakefield!"

On the dance floor, Jessica covered her mouth with her hands in surprise. She accepted the congratulations of her classmates as she glided up to the stage, tears trembling on her lower lashes. She bowed her head and the sparkling crown was placed atop her gleaming blond hair.

"Shall we?" Bruce asked, offering his arm.

Jessica took it, and he led her to the center of the dance floor, where the spotlight followed them as they swayed to the music. Then Bruce tipped her chin up with his finger, and her breath caught in her chest as he leaned down to kiss her. . . .

At that moment, the bell rang, signaling the end of class. Notebook paper tore all around her as everyone stood up to hand in their work. Jessica looked down at her paper. Totally blank.

"Argh. Not again," she said under her breath.

She waited for one of the linebackers from the football team to get in front of her, then snuck behind him until she could slip through the door unnoticed. The moment she was safe in the hall, she sighed with relief. Free at last.

"Don't you just *hate* her?" Lila spat, stepping up next to Jessica as they made their way down the hall.

"Who?" Jessica was still thinking about her daydream.

She absolutely had to win homecoming queen. No question about it. Bruce would have to notice her if he was forced to dance with her.

"Dalton!" Lila screeched. "She just totally humiliated you!"

"Please. It wasn't that bad," Jessica said blithely. "Besides, I think Dalton's kind of cool, usually. For a teacher, anyway."

"Yeah. You wouldn't say that if she was dating *your* father," Lila said, flicking her brown hair over her shoulder.

"Oh, right. Forgot about that. Sorry," Jessica said, biting her lip.

Ms. Nora Dalton had been dating Lila's ridiculously wealthy father for the last few weeks, much to the chagrin of Ken Matthews, Jessica supposed. Of course, everyone in school knew about it, because anything that happened with the wealthy, semifamous Fowler family was big news. Normally, Lila enjoyed all the attention, but this particular story was no fun for her. Jessica knew that Lila hardly ever saw her dad. Now that the man was spending some of his time with Ms. Dalton, it was probably that much harder for Lila to get his attention. Not that Lila would ever admit that.

"It just makes him look so naïve," Lila lamented. "I mean, it's so obvious that she's only after his money."

"Come on, Lila," Jessica said. "Ms. Dalton doesn't

seem like the gold-digger type. Maybe she really likes your dad. He is handsome for, you know, a father."

"Of course he is," Lila snapped. "But why can't she go for someone more her age? It's either my father or Ken Matthews. Isn't there anything in between?"

Jessica snorted a laugh as Lila paused at one of the vending machines near the cafeteria. "Lila, it's not like there's anything actually going on between Ken and Ms. Dalton. It's just stupid rumors."

"Oh, please! I've seen the way she drapes herself across the desk when they're alone in the classroom," Lila said, yanking her wallet out of her bag. "I walked in on them the other day and she was practically shoving her cleavage in his face."

"Aw, Lila! You're jealous! That's so cute," Jessica teased, pinching Lila's cheek.

Lila batted Jessica's hand away and started feeding change into the vending machine. "I'm not jealous. Just because Ken and I are going to the dance together, that doesn't mean I'm in love with him. I just think it's disgusting, that's all."

She selected a Hershey's chocolate bar and crouched in her platform sandals to retrieve it. Jessica smirked. Lila only went for chocolate when she was seriously stressing. If she'd been in her right mind, she would have remembered that chocolate turned her skin all ruddy and gross.

"I just wish I could catch them actually doing something," Lila mused, taking a big bite of the chocolate bar. "Then my father would *have* to dump her."

"Who's dumping who?" Cara asked, her green eyes bright as she came up behind Lila. If there was one thing Jessica could always count on, it was that Cara would be on the lookout for any and all gossip.

"Lila's dad and Ms. Dalton," Jessica answered, feeding change into the drink machine. "Lila's convinced that Dalton and Ken are having an affair, and she wants to expose it so her dad will break up with her."

"What?" Cara practically screeched. "No way. I heard Ken was crushing on her, but are they actually . . . ?"

"Who knows?" Lila asked, biting another chunk off her chocolate bar. "But if there is something going on, I am *so* going to find out."

The second bell pealed just as Jessica's bottled water dropped to the bottom of the machine.

"Gotta go!" Lila trilled. "I don't want to be late for choir. They're picking solo parts for the fall concert today, and I'll just *die* if I don't get one."

"Wait!" Cara reached over and plucked the remaining half of the chocolate bar from Lila's hand. "You'll be more confident if you're not all red in the face."

Lila paused, still chewing. "Oh my God. Jess! Why did you let me eat that?"

Jessica shrugged. "I forgot."

Lila groaned and rushed away, whipping out a compact mirror to check her reflection. Jessica smirked and took a sip of her water as she and Cara started down the hall for her next class.

"Omigod, Jess. You'll never believe what I heard this morning," Cara said, her green eyes wide. She launched the chocolate bar into a garbage can and smacked her hands together. "Dana Larson is going to homecoming with Tom McKay. Is that not the weirdest couple ever?"

"Yeah. Totally weird," Jessica said quickly. "You haven't heard if Bruce has asked anyone yet, have you?"

Cara grinned. "Not yet. Why don't you just ask him already?"

Jessica's heart clenched at the thought. Normally, she wouldn't have a problem asking a guy out, but Bruce was just so . . . intimidating. Not that Jessica would ever admit that to Cara. Sometimes Jess thought he liked her, like when she'd caught him checking her out at Casa del Sol the other day when she was ordering her food. But other times he treated her the way he'd treat any other loser in school. Like the time she'd dropped her books right in front of him and he'd given her a grin and said, "Way to go, Wakefield," before stepping over the mess and walking off.

"I don't ask people out, Cara. They ask me," Jessica

said with a sniff. "Besides, even if he decides to go with someone else, we'll still be spending most of the night together. After we win king and queen."

Cara winced, sucking some air through her teeth as she mounted the stairs to the second floor. "I don't know, Jess. I've actually heard a lot of people are going to vote for Enid."

Jessica's heart sank. "What?"

"She's totally locked up the loser vote," Cara said matter-of-factly, raising her hand. "All the band geeks, literary types, honors society members, skater freaks, goth chicks . . . they all want to see someone unexpected win. The normal freshmen will vote for you because you're captain of the cheerleading squad and it's obvious, but word is the sophomores are behind Lila. They're a little more sophisticated, and they worship her for her clothes and celebrity connections."

"Of course," Jessica said through her teeth.

"Then when it comes to the popular kids in the junior and senior classes, you, Lila and Liz are going to split the vote, so . . . I think Enid really has a chance."

Jessica paced over to the wall, where one of her very own professionally made homecoming posters hung, her mind going fuzzy. This could not be happening. There was just no way that dorky Enid Rollins could beat her out for homecoming queen. It would be the biggest humiliation of Jessica's life. But then, Cara really had her finger on the pulse of the school. If she said the vote was swinging that way, it was pretty solid information.

"No way. There is just no way," Jessica ranted. "You're telling me that Enid Rollins is going to get to dance the spotlight dance with Bruce Patman? That is so wrong! She'll give him hives!"

"Sorry, Jess. That's what I heard," Cara said with a shrug.

"All this just because she started dating Ronnie freaking Edwards? This is so not fair!" Jessica wailed. "She shouldn't have even been nominated."

Cara backed toward class, her eyes pitying. "Sorry, Jess. What can you do? Come on. We're gonna be late."

But Jessica could not make herself move. She pressed her forehead up against the cool cinder-block wall next to the photograph of her own smiling face and tried to control her breathing. This was not going to happen. There was just no way she was going to lose the crown, and her chance with Bruce Patman, to Enid Rollins.

Cara's words echoed in her mind. *Sorry, Jess. What can you do?*

"Something," Jessica said to herself, taking a deep breath. "There's always something I can do."

And with that comforting thought, she finally stood up straight and strode into class, just as the final bell rang.

CHAPTER
3

JESSICA ROUNDED THE corner in the arts wing after seventh period and saw Bruce about to head into the stairwell. Before she could double-think it, she raced over and slipped through the door ahead of him. Fifteen whole seconds trapped in a crowded stairwell with him would be something, at least. Jessica had snagged guys in less time than that.

"Whoa. Where's the fire?" Bruce asked as Jessica brushed by him.

Jessica blinked her big blue-green eyes at him innocently. "Oh, sorry. Didn't see you there."

He snorted a laugh and Jessica practically melted. Even his teeth were perfect. "Right."

And that chin. She'd never seen it from quite this angle before.

"So are we moving or what? There's a line forming, you know," Bruce said.

Blushing, Jessica started up the stairs, knowing full well that Bruce would have a perfect view of her bare legs in her miniskirt as she climbed.

"So, Wakefield. You must be psyched about homecoming court," Bruce said.

"I guess," she said casually, lifting one shoulder as she glanced back at him. "Whatever. It's just an archaic ritual."

"Yeah. Right." Bruce laughed sarcastically. "I bet you'd kill for that crown."

Jessica took a moment to reply. He'd come too close to hitting the nail on the head. "Well, I do like pretty things," she said finally.

"We have that in common," Bruce said with a lascivious smile that turned Jessica's knees to goo. She gripped the banister to keep from tripping. "So, who're you going with?"

Ha! That only took about *five* seconds.

"Actually, I don't have a date yet," she said, pausing and looking down at him as she reached the break in the steps. Her blond hair fell forward, framing her face, and she knew that the particular pose she was striking high-lighted all her best features. "Hard to believe, isn't it?"

Jessica's pause held up the flow of traffic on the stairs, and a couple of people protested, but it was totally worth it. Bruce's eyes raked over her as if he were looking at the latest cover of *Maxim*.

"Yeah. That's a puzzler," he said, semientranced.

Yes! He's mine. He is totally, totally mine!

"Why don't you go with Winston Egbert? He's been licking your feet since kindergarten," Bruce said suddenly.

He slapped her on the shoulder twice, as if she were one of his tennis teammates, and slipped past her, continuing toward the top of the stairs. Jessica's heart dropped like a stone. What had just happened? One second he was looking at her as if he'd like to eat her up with a spoon, the next he was insulting her with Winston Egbert references? No. Not acceptable. She had to get his attention back. She'd been so close. . . .

"Omigod! My necklace!" Jessica gasped, following Bruce to the top of the stairs. She grabbed at the high neckline of her T-shirt, pretending her lavaliere wasn't hidden beneath it. "It must have fallen off on the stairs. Bruce, you have to help me find it. It was a sweet-sixteen present from my parents."

Bruce paused at the door, pushing his back up against it so people could slide through past him. He glanced at the stairs in a cursory way, then shrugged.

"Sorry, Jess. I don't see it. But I'm sure it'll turn up." He gave her another shoulder whack. "Later."

Just like that, he was gone. Jessica gaped after him, completely thrown. Bruce was a gentleman. She'd *seen* him open doors for his dates at school dances, jump to get them punch, take their hands as he helped them from his car. So why the heck did he insist on treating her like one of the guys? It was beyond insulting.

And it only made her want him more. She was going to be one of those girls he treated like a goddess. She just had to figure out how.

"Did I hear you say you lost your necklace?"

Jessica turned around to find Winston himself, looking at her imploringly. His ears were red with embarrassment, probably from the effort of talking to her.

"Eh, whatever. I didn't like it much anyway," Jessica said, waving a hand.

"You're lying. I know how important that necklace is to you. I was there when you got it, remember?" Winston said.

How could she forget? Why Elizabeth had felt the need to invite Winston to their joint sweet-sixteen party was a mystery to her, but there he'd been.

"I'll find it for you, Jess. My mom calls me Eagle Eye. I'm always finding earring backs for her . . . and paper clips . . . and needles . . ."

Jessica would have told him not to bother, but he was already down on his hands and knees on the grimy floor, and he seemed pretty determined. Everyone who passed by him chuckled and laughed, but he didn't seem to notice or care. It was kind of sweet, actually. He was on a mission. For her. So she decided to leave him to it.

"All right, Winston. I have to go. But let me know if you find anything," Jessica told him.

"You got it, Jess!" he called after her.

She rolled her eyes and laughed under her breath as she walked off to class.

• • •

"Is Liz here?" Jessica demanded as she walked into the kitchen that afternoon. Her mother was at the sink rinsing off a head of lettuce. Jessica tossed her messenger bag and cheerleading gear onto a chair at the table.

"Hello to you too," Alice Wakefield said, tossing her blond hair over her shoulder as she looked at her daughter. "And no, she's not home."

Jessica groaned and whipped open the refrigerator to stare at its contents. She'd been in a foul mood ever since her encounter with Bruce that afternoon. Why did he have to be so confusing? All she wanted to do was vent to her sister about it and see what Liz had to say. Dumping her problems on her twin almost always made her feel better. But of course Liz wasn't home. Why was the universe hating her today?

"Where *is* she?" Jessica demanded, pulling out a small bottle of lemonade and popping it open. "I have to talk to her."

"She's out with Enid. I think they're getting homecoming court posters made or something," her mother replied, a concerned line forming between her blue eyes. "Everything okay?"

"No! Everything's not okay," Jessica said, slapping her hand down on the marble countertop. "I mean, she's *my* sister and I need her. Why is she always hanging out with that T.L.?"

"T.L.?" Mrs. Wakefield asked, growing amused.

"Total loser!" Jessica spat.

"Jessica." Her mother gave her a reproving look. "Enid isn't a loser. She's a sweet girl. And she and your sister happen to have a lot in common."

"Yeah, but only because Enid's turning herself into some kind of Liz clone," Jessica groused. "She's always over here, like, worshipping Liz and following her every move. Doesn't she have her own house to go to?"

Alice tossed the lettuce into the salad spinner and sealed the top, then wiped her hands on a towel. "You'd better take it easy, Jess. Your skin is turning green," she joked.

Jessica's jaw dropped. Her pulse started to pound in her ears. "You think I'm jealous? Of Enid Rollins? Please, Mom. Don't insult me."

"Well, Liz has been spending a lot of time with her lately, which means you don't see your sister as much as you're used to." Her mother shrugged. "It makes perfect sense."

"Whatever," Jessica said, rolling her eyes. Her face grew hot and she clenched her free hand into a fist. "Liz can hang out with whoever she wants."

"Good. I'm happy to hear you're so open-minded," Mrs. Wakefield said, spinning the lettuce and stifling a smile.

"I mean, if she wants to associate with known losers who only get nominated for homecoming court because they have hot boyfriends, that is *fine* by me." Jessica grabbed a cherry tomato from the bowl in front of her and popped it in her mouth, crunching into it violently.

"Fine," her mother said.

"I mean, it's not like *I* don't have anyone else to hang out with," Jessica said, taking another tomato. She bit into it and continued to rant, her vehemence slowly rising. "I have tons of friends. Way more than Liz does.

She and Enid could run off together and form a cult for all I care. I don't need either one of them."

Mrs. Wakefield sighed, stopped what she was doing, and came around the counter. She put both hands on Jessica's shoulders and looked her in the eye.

"Jessica, listen to me," she said in a soothing voice. "No one is ever going to replace you as far as Liz is concerned."

Jessica hated when her mother spoke to her that way, as if she were a five-year-old.

"I already told you I don't care!" Jessica said, pulling away. She picked up her lemonade, but her hands were trembling with ire. The bottle slipped, spraying pink liquid all over the front of her white T-shirt. "Omigod! It's totally ruined!" she cried.

Alice sighed again. "Jessica, please calm down. It's just a T-shirt."

"Just my *favorite* T-shirt! You don't understand anything!" Jessica shouted, tears spilling onto her cheeks.

She turned around and fled upstairs, angry at the world. She was about to run into her own room, but it was such a ridiculous mess she couldn't even face it. Instead, she turned toward Elizabeth's pristine bedroom and flung herself on the bed. It took her a good five minutes to calm herself down, but when she did, she felt like an idiot. Her mother was right. She was jealous of Enid Rollins. What kind of universe did she live in where Enid had a boyfriend, a date for homecoming, a real shot at winning homecoming queen, *and* quality time with Liz, while Jessica had none of the above? It was just so wrong.

But there was no reason to freak out about it publicly. Doing that just made her feel like a loser herself. At least her mother was the only one who had witnessed it.

Taking a deep breath, Jessica sat up and dried her eyes. Elizabeth's computer light was blinking, on standby as always, and Jessica pushed herself up, deciding to check her e-mail. Maybe someone sent her a message asking her to the dance. Some guys were shy that way. Not that she preferred guys who couldn't speak up for themselves, but at this point it was looking like she might have to settle.

Jessica woke up the computer and was about to open the Internet connection when she noticed a folder in the middle of the desktop labeled "George." That was odd. Elizabeth didn't know anybody named George as far as Jessica knew. Curious, Jessica double-clicked the folder. Inside were dozens of files that looked like e-mail messages. Jessica opened the first one.

Dear Enid,

It's the one-year anniversary of that night and I can't stop thinking about it. I'm sorry, I just can't. The sirens, the screaming, the flashing lights. That poor kid. That poor, poor kid . . . How could we have let ourselves get so messed up? Who mixes all that stuff? Vodka, E, pot. What were we thinking? I feel so guilty tonight. I wish I could talk to you. I wish I could call you right now. But I know I can't. I promised to give you space.

I'm sorry. I shouldn't even be writing this. None of this was your fault. I just miss you so much and I'm so sorry. I hope one day I can be in the place you're in right now, but I just feel bleak. Anything from you. Just an e-mail. A word. I don't care. It would really help.

I'm sorry, again.

Love,

George

Jessica sat back in Elizabeth's cushy desk chair, dumbfounded.

"Oh. My. God! Enid is a druggie!" Jessica covered her mouth to keep from laughing. Then, with a sudden insatiable need, she quickly opened one e-mail message after another after another. Each one was even better than the last. This George kid got gradually more and more lucid as time went on, until he sounded almost normal, but it was perfectly clear what had happened that night. *And* that George—whoever he was—was head over heels in love with Enid.

Slowly but surely, a wicked idea took shape in Jessica's mind.

There's always something I can do, Cara, she thought triumphantly. *Always something.*

She quickly opened her e-mail and went to the SVH Web site where all student e-mail addresses were listed. Choosing carefully, she selected the five most incriminating e-mails from George she could find and attached them to a brief message.

> Thought you might want to know what your girlfriend is really all about. Call it a public service.

Jessica made sure the e-mails had attached; then she sent the whole thing off to Ronnie Edwards.

CHAPTER

4

"OKAY, WHAT IS up with Ronnie and Enid?" Todd Wilkins asked, glancing over his shoulder at the theater doors to make sure the couple hadn't returned. "Is it tense between them or is it just me?"

"It's not you," Elizabeth confirmed. "He's been acting like a jerk all night."

She sat back in the comfy new stadium-style seat at Valley Cinema, letting it bounce on its hinges. It was Friday night, and the four of them were out on a double date. Unfortunately, during dinner at Casa del Sol, it had been more as though Liz, Todd, and Enid were on a date and they had brought along someone's sulky little brother. Ronnie had barely said a word to anyone all night, except when asked a direct question.

"I know. What's his deal?" Todd asked, his warm brown eyes concerned. "When she offered to help him get popcorn, I think he actually grunted at her."

Elizabeth shivered, pulling her cardigan sweater tighter around her sundress. "I'm sure it's fine. Maybe they're just having an off night," she said casually.

She didn't want Todd to notice how worried she actually was. It seemed like way too much of a coincidence that Ronnie was acting so weird tonight—so soon after Enid had started getting closer to George. Was it possible that Ronnie had somehow found out about the e-mails? Had Enid left one up on her computer screen without realizing it?

"Hey. Are you cold?" Todd asked, shimmying out of his red and white varsity jacket. "Here. They've got the AC cranked so high in here it's out of control."

"Thanks." Elizabeth smiled as he slipped the jacket, still toasty from his body heat, over her shoulders. She looked at his profile as he watched one of the commercials playing up on the screen. He was so handsome. Sometimes Elizabeth still couldn't believe she was lucky enough to be going out with Todd. Especially since Jessica had done practically everything she could think of to keep them apart while she tried to snag Todd for herself. Not that Elizabeth could blame her, really. Todd was one of the hottest guys in school—*the* hottest, in Liz's opinion. And as star of the football and basketball teams, he was totally Jessica's type—on the surface, anyway. But the more Elizabeth got to know him, the more she realized how down-to-earth and caring he was. He didn't care if he was considered cool and popular or not. He talked to anyone and everyone in school and actually listened to what they had to say. He was smart and mature and kind. All of which made him less Jessica's type and more Liz's.

Especially considering that Jessica's current obsession was shallow-as-a-soda-spill Bruce Patman. Todd's polar opposite.

"I just hope Ronnie's not on another jealousy trip," Todd said suddenly. "Remember Guido's that day? When he totally flipped on the waiter for talking to her?"

"Omigod, I know. And they *so* weren't flirting. All Enid was trying to do was make sure there was no garlic on her pizza," Elizabeth said, shaking her head.

"It's like he's suspicious of anyone with testosterone," Todd replied, incredulous. "I know he loves her, so why doesn't he trust her?"

Elizabeth grinned at Todd's innocent indignation. "You are too cute, you know that?"

Todd turned to her and gave her a sexy, lopsided smile. "It's a gift."

Her pulse fluttering, Elizabeth leaned in and brushed the side of his neck with her lips. Todd turned his head and kissed her softly in response. Elizabeth's heart felt as if it were going to jackhammer its way out of her chest. She loved being with Todd so much. Loved how it made her feel giddy and gushy and mature and sophisticated all at once. If they ever broke up, she seriously thought she might die. Literally. She was sure she would not be able to handle it. Which made her think of Enid and how scared she'd been the other night.

Liz pulled back just in time to see Ronnie coming down the aisle. Alone.

"Where's Enid?" she asked him as he dropped down in the chair next to Todd's.

"I don't know. Bathroom?" he said flatly. He grabbed a handful of popcorn and crunched into it, effectively ending any conversation.

Elizabeth shot Todd an annoyed look. "I'm gonna go check on her. Be right back."

She shoved through the doors to the lobby and made a beeline for the bathroom. The harsh fluorescent light inside stung her eyes after the darkness of the theater. Enid was standing at the mirror, wiping smudged eyeliner from under one eye. Her nose was red from crying.

"Enid! Are you okay?" Elizabeth asked.

"Something's wrong, Liz," Enid replied, sniffling. "Ronnie has barely even looked me in the eye all night. I don't even know why he came out with me. Unless he just didn't want to be rude and break plans with you guys." She took a shuddering breath and stared at Liz's reflection in the mirror. "Do you think he knows?"

"How could he? I haven't told anyone, and I know you haven't," Elizabeth assured her, leaning back against the counter so they could face each other. "Maybe he's just upset about something else. Something that has nothing to do with you."

"Maybe," Enid said dubiously.

"Just ask him what's up. Maybe he needs someone to talk to," Elizabeth suggested.

"Or maybe he'll just break up with me," Enid replied, a fresh tear rolling down her cheek.

"He's not going to break up with you. He loves you. And you haven't done anything wrong," Elizabeth said.

"Unless he found out somehow," Enid repeated, her eyes wide. "Liz, what if he found out?"

"Enid, you have to stop stressing out about this," Elizabeth told her firmly. "All you've done is send e-mails to an old friend. And even if he *did* find out about the other stuff, he can't hold it against you. It happened way before you met him. It wouldn't be fair."

Enid nodded. "You're right."

"Just try to calm down and see what happens. If you keep acting all paranoid, he's going to figure out that something's wrong," Liz finished.

"Okay. Okay. You're right." Enid took a deep, cleansing breath and blew it out. She gave herself a bolstering look in the mirror. "You're good at this pep-talk thing, Liz. Maybe you should be the cheerleader instead of Jessica."

"Take that back," Liz joked.

"Sorry! I take it back!" Enid said, raising her hands in surrender. She even smiled, which made Elizabeth feel much better.

"You know, you're probably right," Enid said, touching up her lip gloss. "There's probably just something else bothering him. I am going to be the good girlfriend and listen to him, and everything is going to be okay."

With that, she turned and strode confidently out of the bathroom. Elizabeth followed slowly, just hoping that they were both right.

• • •

Enid stared through the windshield of Ronnie's car as they drove through Sweet Valley in silence. She was so tense, her fingers were gripping the folds of her knee-length skirt into two tight balls in her lap. She stole a glance at Ronnie for the tenth time in as many minutes, but he hadn't budged. His eyes were focused resolutely on the road, his jaw clenched and his expression stony.

"So . . . um . . . how're things going with the dance?" Enid asked tentatively.

"Fine," Ronnie replied.

She cleared her throat and tried again. "That didn't exactly *sound* fine."

Ronnie sighed. "There are budget issues."

"Oh. Well, I'm sure the faculty advisor can help with that, right? And you have Ms. Dalton. Doesn't get much better than that."

"Are you kidding me?" Ronnie finally looked at her, but in a belligerent way. What had she said wrong now?

"What? I think she's cool. For a teacher," Enid replied.

"Yeah. It's really cool to hook up with a student," Ronnie said with a snort. "If that's your definition of cool—"

"Oh, come on. Are you talking about that thing with Ken Matthews?" Enid said incredulously. "That's just a rumor."

"How do you know?" Ronnie demanded.

Enid's face flushed. Ms. Dalton was one of her favorite teachers. Someone she could talk to—and had often talked to—the way she'd talk to a friend. And here

Ronnie was, ready and willing to write her off as some cradle-robbing maniac.

"How do you know it's not?" she shot back.

"Whatever," Ronnie replied, shaking his head. "All I know is, these stories don't just appear out of thin air. They've gotta come from somewhere."

Once again he stared through the windshield, as if he was totally done with the topic. At a loss, Enid held her breath and counted to ten. Normally, she didn't want her dates with Ronnie to end, but tonight she was relieved to see her old Spanish-style house at the corner of her block come into view. In a few minutes she would be home and this horrible night would finally be over.

Except that Ronnie's car blew right by the turn.

"Uh, Ronnie?" Enid said. "That was my street."

"Yeah, I know," he replied, shifting his hands on the wheel. "My parents have this party tonight, so I figured we could go back to my house for a while."

Instantly, Enid's heart surged with hope. He wanted her to come back to his house! He did want to spend time with her. From the way he'd been acting, she would have thought he'd drive by her house, slow down slightly, and shove her out onto the curb before speeding away. But no. He wanted to go back to his empty house, and she knew what that meant. Two minutes ago she'd been near tears, and now she was biting her lip to keep from grinning too wide.

"I guess we could do that," she said, trying to keep her tone light and flirtatious. Maybe she could salvage this situation after all.

Ten minutes later, Enid slipped out of her denim jacket and sat on the leather couch in Ronnie's living room. He dimmed the lights and dropped down next to her. Enid's heart thudded in anticipation. Ronnie was an incredible kisser. All slow and searching and tender. She could kiss him for hours on end. She turned to him, expecting him to tuck her hair behind her ear or kiss her lightly like he always did, but before she could even close her eyes, his mouth was completely smothering her.

Enid tried to kiss him back, but he was moving around roughly and haphazardly, leaning his weight forward as if to push her down on her back. She whacked his shoulder a couple of times and finally pushed him away. He blinked at her, and she could have sworn there was anger and hurt in his eyes. Her heart lurched. What was going on here? Whatever it was, it didn't feel good.

"What's the rush?" she joked, trying to lighten the mood. "I thought we had hours."

"Fine. If you don't feel like it," Ronnie said testily.

He picked up the remote and put on SportsCenter, turning his profile to her. Tears sprang to Enid's eyes. She couldn't take this anymore. She snatched the remote out of his hands and muted the television.

"Okay. What is going on with you tonight?" Enid blurted out.

"Nothing." He grabbed the remote back and turned up the volume. "I guess you're just tired out from giving it up to your buddy George, huh? No energy left for me?"

Enid felt as if the couch had just been yanked out from under her. She gripped the leather arm as if it were the safety bar on a roller coaster.

"What did you just say?" she asked, her mouth dry.

"No, really. I mean, I thought *I* was your boyfriend," Ronnie said sarcastically. "But I guess I'm wrong. Because if I were your boyfriend, you wouldn't need to write love letters to some loser behind my back."

All the air whooshed from Enid's lungs. "He's not a loser," she said automatically.

"Oh, so now you're defending him?" Ronnie demanded, throwing the remote on the table with a clatter that made her breath catch. "And I don't even hear you denying that you're fooling around with the guy!"

"Ronnie, I'm . . . I'm not fooling around with anyone,"

Enid stammered. Her brain was so muddled she could barely decide what to say first. "How did you even find out about him?"

"What does it matter?" Ronnie asked, his blue eyes flashing. "The point is, I know. And I also know what the two of you used to do together. I can't believe what a hypocrite you are. Walking around like you're Miss Prude, and a member of SADD and all that crap. Meanwhile, you're really just a—"

"Do not finish that sentence," Enid said through her teeth, feeling a sudden flash of anger.

For the first time, Ronnie seemed chagrined by what he was about to say. He looked at his feet and took a deep breath. Enid tried to use the moment to collect her thoughts. To calm her out-of-control heartbeat. She had no idea how Ronnie had found out about George, but he was right. At the moment, it didn't matter. All that mattered was making him hear the truth. Making him understand.

"Ronnie, please just let me explain," Enid said quietly, tucking her long brown hair behind her ears. "I know you're angry, but if you would listen to my side of the story, I—"

"I can't, Enid," Ronnie said flatly.

Enid's hopes crumbled. "You can't what?"

"I can't do this." Ronnie looked at her, his eyes almost pleading. "Please just go."

Go? What the heck was he talking about?

"Ronnie—"

"No! You're just like my mom!" Ronnie shouted, standing. His hands curled into fists. "She cheated on my dad for years and lied right to his face. It was pathetic! The way he just believed her. The way he kept taking her back for so long! That's not me. I can't be with a liar, okay? I can't do it!"

Enid was taken aback by the venom in his tone, but she wasn't ready to give up yet. She knew his mother had hurt him. She knew that was the reason he was so distrustful. But she was not his mother. "I'm not a liar, Ronnie," she said. "I've just been trying to turn over a new leaf. I—"

"Well, you're not going to be doing it with me," Ronnie said forcefully. "This is over as of now."

Tears finally spilled onto Enid's cheeks. Her heart felt as if it were tearing down the middle. How could he treat her like this? She loved him so much, and she had thought he loved her. "Ronnie—"

"I'll drive you home if you want," he said, grabbing his keys. He shot her a haughty look. As if he was so mature for being kind enough to offer a lowlife like her a ride. Enid dried her eyes and picked up her jacket.

"You know what? Thanks anyway," she said, speaking past the sob that was lodged in her throat. "I'd rather walk ten miles than get back in the car with you."

She turned around and walked out, crying silently until she was a block away from his house, when she finally sat down on the curb and just let the tears flow.

How did this happen? How could he possibly know about George and everything that happened?

She tried to keep the answer at bay for as long as humanly possible, but finally the obvious truth of it all overtook her. It couldn't be a coincidence that she had told Liz about George less than a week ago. Until then, no one in the world had known about him other than Winston. So either Winston had suddenly decided to blab to Ronnie for no reason, or Elizabeth had told him. There was simply no other explanation.

Maybe Elizabeth told Todd and Todd told Ronnie, Enid thought, trying to give her friend an out. But it didn't even matter. Elizabeth had promised not to tell *anyone*. She knew how fast things got out at SVH. The only way to stop a rumor from spreading like a forest fire was to keep your mouth shut to begin with. And clearly, Liz hadn't been able to do that. She hadn't been able to do that one little thing for her supposed best friend.

Enid's sobs came harder. As she sat there clutching her stomach, doubled over on some random curb in the middle of Ronnie's neighborhood, she couldn't decide which hurt more: Ronnie's venom, or Elizabeth's betrayal.

CHAPTER
5

"WHAT DO YOU think?" Jessica asked, holding up the new black wrap dress she'd bought at the mall earlier that day. She twirled away from her reflection in Elizabeth's full-length mirror and looked at Liz, who was sitting on her bed with Jane Austen's *Emma* open in front of her. "With that gold necklace you got for Christmas?"

Elizabeth raised her eyebrows and glanced up from her book. Her sister was acting even more manic than usual for a Saturday night. "Is that your not-so-subtle way of asking if you can borrow it?" she asked.

"Is that your not-so-subtle way of saying yes?" Jessica asked, already rooting around in Liz's wooden jewelry box.

Elizabeth sighed and rolled her eyes. "Go ahead."

"Cool! I'm gonna take these earrings, too!" Jessica announced giddily, fastening Elizabeth's favorite gold hoops in her ears.

"Where're you going, anyway?" Elizabeth asked suspiciously. She laid her book aside and sat up, crossing her legs. "I thought you were just hanging out with Cara."

"I am, but not at Cara's house," Jessica said, her blue-green eyes mischievous as she stepped out of her shorts and into the dress.

Elizabeth smirked. Her sister loved to play this silly little I-know-something-you-don't-know game. As if they were still in kindergarten. And somehow Jessica always considered herself to be the sophisticated one.

"Whatever," Elizabeth said with a yawn, picking up her book again. She lazily turned the page, knowing how much it would infuriate her twin. "Have fun."

Jessica stopped primping and glared at Liz in the mirror. "Aren't you even the tiniest bit curious about where we're going?"

"Not really," Elizabeth said, scanning the page, which she had already read.

"You mean you're not even going to try to guess?" Jessica asked. She turned around and stared indignantly.

"All right, fine," Elizabeth said, dramatically rolling

her eyes. "You've been invited to a royal ball in London, where Prince William is going to select his new bride from among all the most gorgeous women in the land. Oh yeah! I see your fairy godmother outside right now trying to turn one of the oranges from the tree into a private jet!" she joked, sitting up straight to see out the window.

"You are such a dork," Jessica snapped, laughing nonetheless.

"Okay, fine. I give. Where're you going?" Elizabeth asked.

"Oh, just to an exclusive martini-tasting party at Lila's," Jessica said blithely.

"A martini tasting?" Elizabeth asked.

"Yeah. It's just like a wine tasting, but with martinis," Jessica explained, lifting her palm.

"Uh, I get it. But aren't there a few flaws in that plan?" Elizabeth asked. She reached back to tie her blond hair in a low ponytail.

"What? Like we're underage? Big deal. It's a *tasting*, Liz. You're supposed to swish and spit," Jessica said, fluffing her hair around her face.

"Like anyone there will," Elizabeth replied.

"Well, Lila already invited us all to stay over, so no one will be drinking and driving . . . *Mom*," Jessica said.

"Yeah, yeah." Elizabeth returned to her book.

"Oh, is someone a little depressed that she wasn't invited?" Jessica teased, totally misconstruing Elizabeth's mood. "You could've been if you tried a little harder with Lila, Liz. Or are you happy sitting around on a Saturday night in a pair of ratty sweats reading a book that could put a caffeine addict to sleep?"

"Actually, I *am* perfectly happy this way," Elizabeth said matter-of-factly. "And why would I want try harder with someone who's a totally shallow fake?"

"Liz! That's my best friend you're talking about," Jessica replied, her jaw dropping. "Besides, it's not like she's any more fake than some of your friends."

"Like who?" Elizabeth asked.

"Like Enid," Jessica replied.

Elizabeth dropped her book now. "Why are you so determined to hate Enid? She's always nice to you. And Lila, by the way, is never nice to me. In fact, I wouldn't be going to this thing if I *had* been invited. She's a total snob. Guess that's what happens when your father gives you a platinum card for your fifth birthday."

"Know what else happens? You get to throw fabulous parties and know for sure that all the coolest people are going to be there," Jessica replied, flipping her long blond hair over her shoulder. "Doesn't seem too bad to me."

"All the coolest people?" Elizabeth asked archly. "You mean Bruce Patman, Bruce Patman, and . . . oh yeah, Bruce Patman?"

"Ha ha," Jessica said as she fastened Elizabeth's necklace around her neck. "Yes, if you must know, he *is* going to be there. And he's going to ask me to homecoming if it kills me." She turned around and smoothed the front of her dress. "So, is the dress okay? It doesn't make me look fat, does it?"

"Yes and no," Elizabeth replied.

"What?" Jessica screeched, checking her perfect reflection yet again.

"I meant yes, the dress is okay, and no, it doesn't make you look fat," Elizabeth replied patiently. "Sheesh, Jess. Have an aneurysm, why don't you?"

"I don't know what that is, but I'm positive I don't have one," Jessica joked in reply. She grabbed her clutch purse and twirled on her way out the door. "Later, babe! Have fun with your book. Or, I know, why don't you call Enid Blah-Is-My-Middle-Name Rollins and you can read passages out loud to each other!"

She blew Liz a kiss and closed the door before the pillow Liz flung could hit her in the head. She left behind her pile of discarded clothing, of course. Elizabeth sighed and got up to toss the shorts and T-shirt into her hamper. As she closed the lid, she realized that Enid hadn't returned the two phone calls Liz had made to her earlier that day. Normally, she and Enid spoke a few times on the weekends, and Liz had expected an update on what had happened once Enid had gotten Ronnie alone the night before. Liz's heart gave an extra-hard thump. Maybe something really was wrong.

Grabbing her cell phone from her bag, she settled in at her desk and hit speed dial three for Enid. She picked up on the third ring.

"Hello?" Enid said coolly. Her voice was thick. As if she'd been crying.

"Enid, hey! It's Liz," she said, sitting forward. "Are you all right?"

"I'm fine," Enid responded curtly.

"You don't sound fine," Elizabeth said.

"Gee, I wonder why." Her tone was blatantly nasty.

Elizabeth blinked. What kind of response was that? "Enid, did something happen with Ronnie last night?"

Enid laughed, but in a harsh, sarcastic way. "I'm surprised you have to ask."

"What?" Elizabeth was now officially confused. And alarmed. The person on the other end of the phone did not sound like her best friend at all. "Enid, what happened? You told him everything, didn't you? Oh God. Was he upset?"

"Upset? That's the understatement of the year. He

broke up with me," Enid replied. "And by the way, I'm not the one who told him. He brought it up first."

"What?" Elizabeth asked again, feeling highly inarticulate. It was pretty much the only word she could think of just then. She couldn't wrap her brain around what she was hearing.

"Yeah, I was kind of shocked too," Enid said. "I mean, who could possibly have told him all about the e-mails to George *and* my police record?"

It took a good long minute for Enid's words to sink in, and when they did, Elizabeth felt as if she'd just been hit by a dump truck. "Enid," she said breathlessly. "You don't think that I—"

"What else am I supposed to think?" Enid shouted, causing Elizabeth's heart to completely stop. "You tell me!"

"I . . . I don't know," Elizabeth stammered, too stunned to think straight. "But Enid, you've got to believe me. I never—"

"Why should I believe you, Liz?" Enid asked. "You're the only one who knew about those letters. *The only one!* I confided in you and you totally stabbed me in the back!"

Enid was crying now. Elizabeth could hear her trying to catch her breath. Her heart shattered in her chest.

There had to be some way to make Enid listen to her. Then they could figure out what had happened together.

"Enid, please—"

But just like that, the line went silent. All the gasping for breath and crying stopped. Liz pulled her phone away and looked at the screen. The call was gone. For a long time, she just stared at it, refusing to believe what had just happened. Then, suddenly, her bedroom door opened behind her. Elizabeth's hand flew to her chest.

"Who was that?" Jessica asked.

"I thought you left," Elizabeth blurted out, startled.

"Cara's not here yet, and then I heard you arguing. . . ." Jessica walked in front of Elizabeth and saw the tears in her eyes. "Omigod, Liz! Are you okay? Was it Todd? Did he break up with you? 'Cause I *will* go over there and kick his—"

"No! It wasn't Todd. It was Enid," Elizabeth said.

"Enid? What was her problem?" Jessica asked, going from indignant to exasperated in record time. "Oh, don't tell me. You forgot to tell her what to wear to bed tonight and she was so upset that she had to call for your advice?"

"Jess! Please!" Elizabeth snapped, her face growing hot. "It's not funny. She was freaking out. She and Ronnie broke up and she's blaming it on me."

"What? Why?" Jessica asked.

Elizabeth stood up and paced across the room to her window overlooking quiet Calico Drive. Her mind was doing a tailspin. None of this made any sense.

"Basically, she told me something that only I was supposed to know. Then Ronnie found out about it and broke up with her, so she's assuming I told him, but I didn't," Elizabeth explained. "I would never do that to her."

"Of course you wouldn't," Jessica said, her beautiful face screwing up in consternation. "Doesn't she know you at all? You're like a nun or something."

"Gee, thanks," Liz said.

"Whatever. I just meant people could confess murder to you and you'd never tell anyone," Jessica said, shrugging. "If she doesn't know that about you, then she's not a very good friend. I bet she just let whatever this secret is slip out herself and now she feels stupid and needs someone to blame it on."

Elizabeth looked at Jessica doubtfully. "That doesn't sound like Enid." She took a deep breath and let it out slowly. "In fact, she didn't sound like herself on the phone, either. She's probably just so upset about breaking up with Ronnie she doesn't even know what she's thinking."

"That's no reason to yell at you till you're on the verge of tears!" Jessica exclaimed.

Elizabeth laughed and turned away from the window. "I'm not on the verge of tears. I'm fine. I'm just worried about Enid."

Jessica snorted a laugh. "And the Nobel Peace Prize goes to . . . I mean, God, Liz. Don't you ever want to fight back?"

"All I want to do is figure out what happened. I just hope I can get Enid to talk to me," Liz said, sitting down on the edge of her bed and looking forlornly at the phone. "If I call her back now, she'll probably hang up on me."

"So give her some time to cool off. Talk to her on Monday," Jessica said in a very even voice.

"Said the girl who can't wait two minutes for her bread to toast," Elizabeth joked.

"Hey. My time is precious," Jessica joked back, flipping her hair behind her shoulder.

Elizabeth chewed her lip. "I'm so mad at Ronnie. How could he break up with her over this? It was all in her past. It had nothing to do with them."

"Well, whatever it is, I'm sure Ronnie had a good reason," Jessica said. "I mean, some secrets are just too big for a couple to get over."

"I guess," Elizabeth said.

"I *know*," Jessica replied.

"Jess, you don't even know what the secret *is*," Elizabeth admonished.

"No. But I can imagine," Jessica said quickly. "And I'm sure that whoever told Ronnie about Enid was probably doing him a big favor."

"You're only saying that because you don't like her," Elizabeth replied, brushing Jessica off. "I just don't understand who could have told him. Who would have done something like that?"

At that moment, Cara's horn honked out in the driveway and Jessica was out the door. "See ya later, Liz! Feel better!" she called over her shoulder.

Two seconds later the front door slammed, and Elizabeth was left alone with her confused, morose thoughts.

How the hell did Ronnie find out? she wondered. *And how am I going to make Enid talk to me?*

CHAPTER

6

"HAVE YOU TRIED the mango-tini?" Lila asked Jessica, giggling as she sipped an orangey pink drink. Her brown hair was back in a sleek ponytail, and she wore a white halter dress that showed off her perfected-in-Cabo tan. "It's, like, yum!"

Jessica laughed and shook her head. "You, Lila Fowler, have not been swishing and spitting."

"Take a look around, Jess! It's a party!" Lila said, waving the glass and spilling half its contents onto the antique rug at their feet. "No one's swishing and spitting!"

Lila had a point. The entire first floor of her palatial mansion was packed with kids from school—juniors and seniors, mostly—and they were all getting louder and rowdier by the moment. Some were even getting messy, which made Jessica wrinkle her nose in distaste. She took the glass from Lila's hand, ostensibly to take a sip, but more to stop Lila from sinking to the level of her guests and doing something she'd regret—like dumping the rest of the martini all over her shoes. Or worse, Jessica's shoes. She was feeling charitable tonight, high from her success with Ronnie and Enid, so she figured she'd help her best friend out.

"Maybe you should take a little break," Jessica suggested. She took a sip of the mango-tini and licked her lips. "That *is* good. You can't even taste the alcohol."

"Well, Esteban is the best martini man in L.A.," Lila trilled waggling her fingers at the bartender across the room. He lifted his chin in response and kept shaking those martinis. "The Fowlers only hire the best."

"I still can't believe your father let you have a party like this while he's away," Jessica said, placing the martini on the glass coffee table in the center of the huge sunken living room.

A tiny frown creased Lila's forehead. "I just told him I was having a few friends over. It's not like he really cares. We could burn the whole damn house down and I'd have time to get it rebuilt before he even set foot in it again."

Jessica's heart twinged for her best friend. "Hasn't been around much lately, huh?"

"Are you kidding? Between the new hotel in Santa Barbara and running all over the place with Ms. Dalton, I haven't seen him in—" Lila glanced at Jessica and blushed. "I mean, my father is a very busy man. He has things to do. And I don't need a babysitter."

She grabbed back the martini glass and finished the rest of the drink in one smooth gulp.

"Omigod, you guys!" Cara called out, dodging the klatches of friends and smooching couples. She grabbed Jessica's wrist, her eyes bright with the excitement of what could only be fresh gossip. "Have you heard about Ronnie and Enid?" she stage-whispered.

"Yeah. He totally dumped her," Jessica said, enjoying the fact that she actually knew some gossip before Cara did.

Cara's face fell briefly at having her moment stolen, but she quickly recovered. "I can't believe he even came tonight," she said. "He looks so depressed."

She stood next to Jessica and looked across the room, folding her slim arms over the front of her kiwi green dress. Jessica followed her gaze and saw Ronnie standing near the marble fireplace on his own, holding a soda, of all things, and staring out the back window-wall at the palm trees swaying in the breeze. Didn't the guy even know this was a party? Didn't he realize he'd just unloaded the most boring girlfriend in history?

"I know. He's totally harshing my vibe," Lila said airily. "Someone should tell him to get over himself. He's lucky I even invited him!"

"So lucky," Cara agreed. She turned and grinned at Jessica. "Why don't you go cheer him up, Jess? Nothing gets a guy over a breakup better than a little dose of Wakefield."

"I appreciate the compliment . . . I think," Jessica said. "But no thanks. I don't need Enid Rollins's sloppy seconds." Besides, Ronnie might have been semicute, but she was saving herself for someone more important. And a lot hotter.

"If you're waiting for Bruce Patman, it's gonna be a long night," Lila offered, reading Jessica's mind. She grabbed a green martini off a passing tray and sipped it. "He's not coming."

Jessica's heart plummeted. "What? Why?"

"He called earlier. Said he had some *thing* at SVU. Fund-raiser or some crap," Lila said, rolling her eyes. "His dad's always giving the school money to build another boring library wing, and every time he does, Bruce gets set up with some trust-fund college chick and goes in to pose for the cameras."

"Some trust-fund college chick?" Jessica echoed.

"Yeah, only this time it's not just any college chick. It's Jenna Malkin of the Boston Malkins," Lila said, putting on a haughty, low voice. "Their families go way back, and she's at SVU now. Those two have been hooking up on and off since sixth-grade summer camp, so I guess they're hooked up again. I heard he's taking her to homecoming, too. Sorry, Jess."

Lila gulped her drink, not looking sorry at all. Meanwhile, Jessica's face burned as she looked down at her new dress and sandals. All this trouble, and for what? So that Bruce could squire some toothy trust-fund chick to *her* homecoming? What the hell was she supposed to do now?

Well, there's always plan B, Jessica thought, glancing over at Ronnie again. Now that Enid had been dumped, there was a very good chance the weepy loser wouldn't even go to the dance. Which meant that Jessica would be the front runner for homecoming queen. Which meant that she and Bruce would get that spotlight dance together. Now all Jessica needed was a date. And thanks to Enid's drama-filled e-mails and one tiny click of the Forward button, there was one very available, semicute, and vulnerable boy left to ask.

"I'll be back in a sec," Jessica said, rolling her shoulders back and homing in on Ronnie.

"Watch out, Ronnie," Cara joked under her breath.

Jessica smirked as she wove her way through the room, sidestepping tipsy girls and loudmouthed guys. She slipped next to Ronnie and put her chin on his shoulder from behind. He started a bit but didn't move.

"Everything okay over here?" Jessica asked in a low, sexy voice.

"Yeah. Fine," Ronnie said flatly.

Jessica walked around in front of him and leaned against the mantel, crossing her legs at the ankle. She saw Ronnie's eyes flick down and tried not to smile too brightly. This was going to be way too easy.

"What's the matter, Ronnie?" she asked. "It's a party. You should be having fun."

"Yeah. This is a great time," Ronnie looked around with a sneer of disgust. "Watching a bunch of people I barely know and hardly like get wasted. I don't even know why I came here."

God. Could he be any more of a downer?

"I think I do," she said, moving a bit closer to him. "I think you came here because you know that old saying. What is it? 'Living well is the best revenge'?" She smiled up at him through her lashes, and Ronnie's eyes shot straight to her cleavage. So, *so* easy. "Come on, Ronnie," she said, taking his hand. "Let's dance."

"Actually, I think I'm just gonna go," Ronnie said, pulling his fingers away.

Jessica felt a white-hot flash of anger. How rude could he be? And did he not realize how lucky he was that she'd even come over here? She stepped in front of him again as he turned to go, putting one hand on her hip.

"Well, I know I'm no Enid Rollins, but you don't have to just blow me off," she said slyly.

"I don't want to talk about Enid," Ronnie said, his eyes smoldering. "I don't even want to think about her." Jessica's heart skipped an excited beat. Actually, when his eyes smoldered like that, he was pretty damn handsome.

"Then come on. I'll distract you," Jessica said.

She reached for his hand again, and this time he barely hesitated. He followed her into the center of the living room, where a few drunken couples were swaying back and forth to the music being piped in through hidden speakers. Jessica slid her toned arms around Ronnie's neck and pressed her body against his. Ronnie's eyebrows shot up quickly, but he didn't flinch. With Jessica taking the lead, they started to step back and forth.

"So, Ronnie . . . what are you going to do now?" Jessica asked casually. "About the dance, I mean?"

"What about it?" Ronnie asked. "All the planning's pretty much done."

"Not the planning," Jessica said with a smile. "I mean what are you going to do about a date?"

Ronnie sighed audibly and lifted his shoulders, letting them drop almost violently. "I don't know. It's too late to find someone now. I'll probably just go alone."

"Come on! The head of the homecoming dance committee can't go to the dance alone," Jessica protested, amused. Then she adopted a serious, wistful expression. "Of course, a member of the court like me shouldn't *not* have a date either, but . . ."

Ronnie blinked and pulled his head back slightly to see her better. His breath smelled like Altoids and cola. Which, when she thought about it, was actually preferable to martini breath.

"Wait a minute. You don't have a date?" he asked.

Jessica shrugged as if it were just as baffling to her. "Nope."

"Well, uh . . . ," Ronnie stammered, his face growing blotchy and red.

"Well, uh, what?" Jessica asked, pressing herself a little bit closer.

"What if we . . . uh . . . went together?" Ronnie asked quickly. "As friends, you know? Since we don't have dates."

Jessica smiled slowly. Too, *too* easy. "I guess that makes sense. Since we don't have dates."

Ronnie's grin was so bright Jessica could hardly look at it without her shades. "Cool."

"Cool," she replied with a nod.

Over his shoulder, Jessica saw Cara shaking her head and smiling while Lila rolled her eyes and finished her green martini—then practically fell onto the white couch behind her.

"Oops. Looks like Lila's getting a little sloppy," Jessica said with an apologetic smile, pulling away from Ronnie. "I'd better go see if I can help."

"Oh. Okay. That's nice of you," Ronnie said, looking impressed.

Jessica shrugged one shoulder, playing it up. "You've gotta be there for the people you love, right?" *Unlike some people we both know,* she added silently.

She saw a cloud pass through Ronnie's expression, and she knew her message had hit home. Enid hadn't been there for him at all. She'd been writing to another guy behind his back. But Jessica . . . Jessica was the kind of girl who cared about her friends. At least, that was what Ronnie was seeing.

"Right," he said finally, forcing a smile.

Jessica started to walk away but paused and looked at

Ronnie over her shoulder. "Oh, by the way. I'm allergic to gardenias, but I absolutely adore orchids. Just don't get me a pink one. I'll be wearing a red dress."

Ronnie nodded, almost stunned, as Jessica sauntered away. She smiled mischievously as she rejoined her friends. Mission accomplished.

CHAPTER
7

ELIZABETH APPROACHED HER homeroom on Monday morning, scanning the hallway for Enid. Normally, if they didn't meet up outside before school, then Enid would definitely be waiting for Liz by her locker. But today, she hadn't been in either place. After the totally insane fight on Saturday and the silence of Sunday, Liz hadn't fully expected her to be around, but she still felt crushed by her absence.

Instead of finding Enid, however, Elizabeth found a big crowd of people standing outside Ms. Dalton's room. The door was closed and there were no lights on inside. Everyone around the door was whispering in urgent tones. Instantly, Elizabeth's reporter's nerves started to sizzle.

"What's going on?" she asked.

"Ms. Dalton's late," Olivia Davidson explained, her brown eyes concerned. She pushed her auburn curls behind her ear, her bamboo bracelets clicking together. "She's never late."

"Probably slept through her alarm after a late night out doing God knows what with Ken," Caroline Pearce joked.

"Oh, you know what they were doing," Guy Chesney said, bumping fists with one of his friends.

A few people laughed, but Elizabeth's jaw dropped. "You guys are sick."

"Oh, please, Liz," Caroline said, flicking her red hair back from her face. "Don't be such a prude. Everyone knows they're doing it."

More laughter. Elizabeth's face burned.

"There's no way Ms. Dalton would fool around with a student," Elizabeth said, clutching the strap on her backpack. "I mean, he's a *kid*. She's not the type."

"Ken Matthews isn't your average kid," Caroline pointed out. "I mean, would you really blame her? I don't know any girl who'd say no to *that*."

Her little gaggle of friends cackled with laughter.

Elizabeth attempted to swallow against a lump that was forming in her throat. She couldn't believe her classmates could be so crass.

"It actually kind of makes sense, when you think about it," Olivia piped up. "Ms. Dalton is reaching her sexual prime, and men her own age are practically burned out. It's a primal law of nature that a fertile woman would seek out the strongest seed."

That got the loudest roar of laughter yet. Olivia's creamy skin turned pink and she looked at Elizabeth, confused. Liz smiled wanly. Olivia had always been heavily into nature and the environment and animal rights, and she lived for biology class. To her, this type of thing was black-and-white. She had no idea how hilarious her peers would find her simple statement of biological fact.

"Even if it does make *biological* sense," Elizabeth said loudly, "I just don't see it. Ms. Dalton is a good person. She's, like, one of the few teachers in this school who actually cares about us—"

"Cares about some of us more than others," Caroline said.

"Do you ever shut up?" Elizabeth demanded.

"Oooh!" a few kids intoned.

"It's not my fault you're too big of a baby to handle

the truth," Caroline replied. "Look at the facts. Ms. Dalton looked horrible all last week, with the limp hair and the big sad eyes and the verge-of-tears crap. She even forgot to give us our weekly quiz in French on Friday. And now she's late. Why would she be so out of it if it weren't true?"

"Gee, I don't know," Elizabeth said sarcastically. "I think I'd be out of it if hundreds of people were spreading lies about me."

"Or maybe she's just upset about something else," Lois Waller piped up, clutching her books to her chest in her usual shy way. "Maybe someone in her family just died."

"Yeah, or maybe she's about to get fired," Caroline replied vehemently. "There's no way Chrome Dome Cooper is going to let a scandal like this get out."

"Whatever," Elizabeth said, checking down the hall for any signs of their teacher. Everyone else was already inside their homerooms, settling in. "I think it'll all blow over since it's completely untrue."

"Maybe you should just ask her if it's true or not," Caroline teased. "You are the star reporter for the Oracle aren't you? Sounds like a lead story to me."

"Maybe you could even sell it to *Maxim* and *Playboy*," Guy joked. "Do you think Ms. Dalton would pose for a pictorial?" he asked, waggling his eyebrows.

"That's it," Elizabeth said, fed up. "I'm going down to the office to see if someone can let us in."

The rest of the students grumbled as Elizabeth pushed herself away from the wall, but she didn't have to go far. The object of their heated discussion had just come around the corner herself. Usually coiffed to perfection, Ms. Dalton looked as if she'd just rolled out of bed. Her dark hair was back in a messy ponytail, and aside from a touch of lip gloss, she was completely makeup free.

"Hi, kids," she said breathlessly. "Sorry I'm late."

She fumbled for her keys as the crowd parted to let her by. She finally got the door open and flipped on the lights. Elizabeth and the rest of the class surged forward to enter the room, but Guy tripped right over Ms. Dalton, who had stopped in her tracks.

"Oh my God," she said, sounding terror-stricken.

Elizabeth's heart fell through her shoes. Taped to the board was a huge photograph of two people in bed. Ken's and Ms. Dalton's faces had been Photoshopped onto the naked bodies. Somehow, someway, someone had found a picture of Ms. Dalton licking her lips with her eyes closed, while Ken was laughing giddily.

Caroline laughed and Elizabeth reached back to smack her arm, hard.

"Ms. Dalton—" Elizabeth said, feeling sick.

"Get rid of it," Ms. Dalton said shakily, turning to

Elizabeth with wet eyes. "Please, just get rid of it. I'll be . . . right back."

Then she turned and strode from the room. Seconds later, they all heard her high heels click-clacking their way down the hall at top speed.

• • •

After third period, Elizabeth made her way back to the foreign-language wing to see if the rumors she'd heard all morning were true—that Ms. Dalton had never returned to her classroom. The health teacher, Mr. Crowe, had subbed during homeroom, but Liz had hoped that her teacher was just gathering herself and would be back. Liz felt sick about what had happened, and it had only gotten worse. The Dalton-Ken pic had been e-mailed to every single student account at SVH, and it looked a lot more real in the smaller, digital form. Everyone was talking about it, passing around PDAs and printouts to show it to their friends. It was a total nightmare. All Elizabeth wanted to do was tell Ms. Dalton she was sorry, or ask if there was anything she could do, or something. She had a feeling she would never forget the haunted, desperate look in her teacher's eyes when she'd asked Liz to get rid of that sick poster. And now it was just everywhere.

Liz was just about to turn the corner before the French classroom when she saw Enid at the water fountain and hesitated. Crap. She had to deal with this first. When had life gotten so utterly complicated?

Taking a deep breath, Elizabeth stepped up next to Enid. Her heart was pounding in her throat. She could hardly believe that the idea of talking to her best friend could make her so insanely nervous.

"Hey," she said tentatively.

Enid stood up, wiped a drop of water from her lip, and tried to walk around Elizabeth.

"Enid, you have to stop avoiding me," Elizabeth said desperately, blocking her friend's path. "We have to talk."

"I have nothing to say," Enid replied icily. She lifted the strap on her messenger bag over her shoulder and then clung to it as if it were a life preserver.

"Enid, you're my best friend. I would *never* talk about you behind your back," Elizabeth said. "You have to believe me."

"Right. Okay. So, what? Your room is bugged or something?" Enid asked, her green eyes flashing.

"Come on, Enid," Elizabeth said, growing frustrated. "Why can't you just trust me?"

"I did trust you, Liz. I did! And look where it got me," Enid said. "Ronnie dumped me and it's all your fault."

"No, it's not!" Elizabeth cried. "God, Enid! What's the matter with you? Did you even ask him if I told him or not?"

"I tried, but he was too busy throwing me out of the house to answer," Enid replied angrily.

"Well, maybe if I talk to him . . . find out what really happened—"

"I have a better idea," Enid snapped. "How about you try keeping your big mouth shut?"

Elizabeth pulled back, her face on fire. She felt as if she'd just been slapped. Enid used the moment of stunned silence to finally get around Liz and speed-walk down the hall, ducking behind her thick hair. It took Elizabeth a full minute to catch her breath. She could not believe that Enid had just talked to her like that. She'd had no idea her friend was capable of such anger. Slowly, Elizabeth turned toward the water fountain, suddenly feeling the need to cool down.

Cara Walker was standing right next to it, her eyes wide with unmistakable glee.

"Hi, Liz!" she said brightly.

Elizabeth groaned in frustration. "Cara, whatever you just heard—"

"I didn't hear anything, Liz. Nothing at all!" Cara trilled.

Then she took off toward the gym as if her feet were on fire.

● ● ●

"What do you think Elizabeth did to break them up?" Caroline asked her friends as they walked right past Elizabeth and Jessica's table at lunch. "Do you think she fooled around with Ronnie behind Enid's back?"

Elizabeth squeezed her apple so hard her fingernails made four tiny crescent moons in the red skin. Jessica's hand darted across the table and covered Liz's.

"Don't listen to them, Lizzie," Jessica said. Then she turned around in her seat and added loudly, "Caroline's just bitter because she doesn't have her own love life to talk about!"

Caroline turned beet red and her friends all laughed before she shot them some serious death glares. Jessica turned around again, proud.

"You're welcome," she said happily, flicking her hair back.

"Jess, do you realize you practically just confirmed to them that I *did* fool around with Ronnie?" Elizabeth asked, feeling exhausted.

Jessica's beautiful face fell. "Oh. Sorry."

"Whatever," Elizabeth said.

She rested her head in her hand and toyed listlessly with her macaroni and cheese. At least it was a gorgeous, sunny day outside. Perfect for sitting at the outdoor picnic tables and getting some fresh air. Of course, the entire student body was doing the same, which meant that all around her, Liz could hear happy voices and laughter. And her name, Ronnie's, and Enid's uttered together quite a bit. All thanks to the motormouth of information that was Cara Walker.

"Between this and the Dalton-and-Ken thing, these jerks are in trash-talk heaven," Liz muttered.

"Don't worry, Liz," Jessica said, taking a bite of her sandwich. "Like you always say, these things blow over."

"I just wish I didn't feel so helpless," Elizabeth said with a sigh. "How am I going to make her listen to me?"

"Well, obviously she's too stubborn," Jessica said. "You've already tried, like, a *million* times."

"Or twice," Elizabeth said wryly. Her sister had a penchant for exaggeration.

"I know!" Jessica said, sitting up straight. "Why don't I talk to her for you?"

"You?" Elizabeth said. "You don't even like her. Why would you do that?"

"Wow. Excuse me for breathing, Liz. I was just

offering to help," Jessica said petulantly. "I hate it when you're so depressed, that's all."

"Would you really talk to her?" Elizabeth asked, lifting her head. "Maybe if you can convince her to hear me out . . ."

"Of course!" Jessica said, lifting her palms. "Whatever you need."

Elizabeth bit her lip and pondered the idea. "Well, I guess it couldn't hurt, right? It's all so screwed up already, nothing could really make it worse."

Not even you, she added silently. Elizabeth knew very well that Jessica normally had an ulterior motive when offering her assistance with anything. But she couldn't think of anything Jessica could gain from talking to Enid on her behalf.

"Thanks for the vote of confidence," Jessica said sarcastically.

Instantly, Elizabeth felt guilty for questioning her sister's motives. "Sorry. I didn't mean it that way," she said quickly. "I know you just want me to feel better."

"I do!" Jessica said, smiling again. "Leave it to me, Liz. I'll bring Enid right around." Her blue-green eyes suddenly widened and she stood up from the table. "There she is now!"

Elizabeth turned around and, sure enough, saw Enid

walking back up toward school from the parking lot with a bag from her favorite deli. Her heart took a leap that was half from dread, half from excitement.

"You're going to talk to her now?" Elizabeth asked.

"Why not get it over with?" Jessica asked, smoothing her shirt. "Don't worry, Liz. I am *all* over this one."

She strutted off after Enid, full of determination, and Elizabeth suddenly felt the tiniest twinge of doubt.

Call this off. Don't let Jessica make things worse, a little voice in her mind told her. *You know how she is.* She opened her mouth to call her twin back, but it was too late. Jessica had already cornered Enid and was gabbing away. All Elizabeth could do now was hope that she'd done the right thing.

CHAPTER
8

JESSICA COULD BARELY hide her distaste as she approached Enid. The girl was sitting on the front steps of the school alone, eating a huge hoagie-style sandwich, wearing an oversized sweatshirt and zero makeup. Didn't she know that a girl was supposed to look her most drop-dead gorgeous during the days after a big breakup? She was supposed to be showing Ronnie how very easy it would be to live without him, show him what he was missing, flirt with every guy she could possibly find. Instead, she looked like a pathetic, lonely slob who couldn't even figure out how to use a mascara wand.

Elizabeth so doesn't need this troll dragging her down,

Jessica thought resolutely. *I am definitely doing the right thing.*

She put on her brightest, most sympathetic smile and waved. "Hey, Enid!"

Enid looked up, and a glob of mayo plopped into her lap. So disgusting.

"What do you want?" she asked Jessica belligerently.

Jessica paused. This girl should feel lucky that anyone was talking to her, let alone Jessica. But she couldn't walk away in a huff. She had a purpose here.

"I just wanted to see how you were doing," Jessica said, her brow creasing as she brushed off the step next to Enid and sat down. "I can't imagine how humiliating it must feel, you know, getting dumped."

Enid glowered. Not a good look for her. "Oh, because you've never been dumped?"

Jessica thought about it for a moment. "No. Actually. I haven't."

"I guess Liz told you everything, then, huh?" Enid asked, putting her sandwich aside.

"Of course she did! All about George and the e-mails and *your arrest,*" she whispered, as if it was just too awful to say out loud. "We tell each other everything. We're *best friends,*" she added pointedly.

Enid scoffed, her cheeks turning pink. She looked at

the toes of her ratty sneakers and hugged her knees. "That's pretty obvious."

And don't you forget it, Jessica thought.

"You shouldn't be so hard on her," Jessica cajoled. "I'm sure she didn't mean to hurt you. You know how these things are."

"I guess I don't," Enid snapped, looking up. "I don't go around stabbing my best friends in the back like some people."

"Oh, come on, Enid," Jessica said. Suddenly, she felt genuinely annoyed. Where did Enid get off talking about Elizabeth like that? Her twin had done nothing wrong. But, of course, Jessica didn't want her to know that. "I'm sure she didn't mean to tell Ronnie," Jessica insisted, remembering her plan. "It probably just slipped out."

"Oh! The most major secret in my entire life just slipped out?" Enid blurted out. "Is that what she told you?"

Jessica widened her eyes, as if snagged. "No! She didn't tell me that. I . . . uh . . . I just—"

"Omigod! Stop trying to defend her!" Enid said, grabbing her sandwich and shoving it back into its paper bag. "I can't believe she sent you of all people to do her dirty work, on top of everything else."

Jessica's eyes narrowed at the comment, but she let

it slide. "Well, she's really upset! You won't even talk to her!"

"She's upset? *She's* upset! What about me? I'm the one who got dumped, remember? She still has Todd and a date for homecoming, and I've got nothing," Enid said. "I'm not even going to the dance now."

Jessica's heart fluttered with excitement. "You're not?"

"A member of the homecoming court without a date?" Enid scoffed. "Thanks, but I've had all the humiliation I can handle for one week."

Inside, Jessica was doing a happy little dance. So much for her main competition. But on the outside, she put on her most pitying expression.

"Come on, Enid. It's not that bad. I'm sure no one actually believes all that stuff Ronnie's been saying about you," she said sweetly.

Enid's entire face crumpled. She was so pale Jessica could practically see through her. That was what happened when a girl didn't even bother with blush.

"What has he been saying about me?" she asked in a hoarse whisper.

Jessica bit her lip. "Actually, it's probably better that you haven't heard."

"Oh my God. I don't believe this. He must really hate me," Enid said, her green eyes filling with tears.

"Well, at least you still have George," Jessica said with a happy shrug.

"I don't have George, Jessica," Enid said angrily, grabbing her things and standing. She hugged all her stuff to her chest—the bag, her books, her soda, and her sandwich. "I don't have Ronnie or George or Liz anymore. I have no one."

"Well, if you ever need to talk . . . ," Jessica offered, barely able to stop herself from laughing.

"Yeah. I'm sure that'll happen," Enid said. "Thanks anyway."

Then she turned around and trudged off, her head bent and her shoulders forward. Jessica stared after her, keeping the sympathetic face on until the girl was through the doors. Then she leaned back on her elbows and stretched her legs out in the sun, feeling very satisfied with herself. This had to be her most perfect plan ever. In one fell swoop she had saved Elizabeth from a totally unsavory best friend, gotten Ronnie out of a potentially embarrassing and explosive relationship (everyone knew addicts eventually relapsed), and taken Enid out of the running for homecoming queen. She wondered if she could major in scheming in college. If so, Liz wasn't going to be the only twin coming home with straight As.

Jessica sighed, already feeling the weight of the home-coming queen crown on her head.

"Bruce Patman," she whispered slyly, "here I come."

● ● ●

Elizabeth was sitting at her desk that night, attempting to concentrate on her English homework, when Jessica's cell phone rang. It was sitting on her desk where Jess had left it earlier, along with half her books and notebooks. Liz grabbed it and paused. The name on the caller ID was "Ronnie E." Suddenly, her pulse was pounding in her temples. Why would Ronnie Edwards be calling Jessica?

"Jess! Your phone!" Elizabeth shouted.

"What?" came Jessica's muffled reply. She had her stereo turned up to a deafening volume.

Elizabeth rolled her eyes and shoved away from her desk. She pushed open the door to Jessica's room with some effort, since there was a mountain of clothes be-hind it. Jessica was dancing around her room, flinging her hair and shaking her hips Shakira style.

"What are you doing?" Elizabeth shouted.

"Tension release!" Jessica replied. "You should try it!"

Elizabeth had no idea what Jessica could possibly be

tense about, but she let it go. "Your phone was ringing," she said, holding out the little pink cell. "I think it went to voice mail."

Jessica stopped dancing and shoved her hair away from her face. "Oh. Thanks," she said breathlessly. "Who was it?"

"Ronnie Edwards." Elizabeth crossed her arms over her chest. "Why would Ronnie Edwards be calling you?"

"We're going to homecoming together," Jessica said, tossing the phone onto her bed. "Did I not tell you that?"

"What? No, you didn't tell me that!" Elizabeth exclaimed. "Jessica! Enid's going to die!"

"Who's being dramatic now, Liz?" Jessica asked, walking over to her mirror to smooth her hair. Elizabeth, meanwhile, killed the music. She was having trouble thinking straight with all the noise.

"Jessica, I don't understand. Do you even *like* him?" Elizabeth asked.

"He's okay," Jessica said with a shrug. "But I'm not going with him for me. I'm going with him for Enid."

Elizabeth blinked. "Okay . . . explain?"

Jessica groaned, as if it were *so* obvious. "Ronnie wasn't going to go to the dance at all after what happened. But I convinced him that he had to go, since he's head of the dance committee and everything. I figure as long as he's there, maybe we can figure out a way to get him and Enid to dance together. Once they're all dressed up and glamorous and dancing under the twinkling lights . . . I'm sure it'll all work itself out."

"That's your plan," Elizabeth said dubiously.

"It could be so romantic!" Jessica said brightly. She dropped onto her stomach on her bed and rested her chin in her hands. "True love conquers all."

"So you're going to the dance with a guy you barely like just to help Enid?" Elizabeth said, standing in front of her sister and fixing her with her most penetrating stare. "Somehow I don't see it."

"What? I felt bad that I couldn't get Enid to talk to you, so I figured this was the next best thing," Jessica said, sitting up. She looked Elizabeth right in the eye as she continued. "If she's back with Ronnie she'll be happy, and then maybe she'll forgive you. I'm doing this for you, Liz."

Elizabeth took a deep breath, finally relenting. She sat down on the edge of the messy bedspread and sighed. Her heart was so heavy she felt as if it were weighing her whole body down. "Well, thanks, but I'm not sure it's going to work. Enid took one look at me in gym class and almost started crying. She totally hates me."

"Well, she did say some pretty harsh stuff when we

talked," Jessica said, shaking her head. "That girl really has her trucker language down."

"Oh God. Don't even tell me," Elizabeth said. "I wouldn't care as much if I'd actually done anything to deserve it. I just don't understand what happened."

"Well, she's always been jealous of you, Liz," Jessica said matter-of-factly. "She was probably just waiting around for an excuse to talk crap about you."

"That doesn't sound like Enid," Elizabeth said morosely.

"Fine. Don't believe me," Jessica said, suddenly offended. She shoved herself off the bed and crossed to her open and quite chaotic closet. "I'm just trying to help, but if you're not even going to *believe* me—"

"I'm sorry, Jess," Elizabeth said, trying to cut the rant short. She was not in the mood to deal with a long one. All she wanted to do just then was curl up in bed and sleep.

"How sorry?" Jessica asked in a leading way, fingering the skirt of the red dress she'd bought for the dance.

Oh God. Here it comes, Elizabeth thought.

"What do you want, Jessica?" she asked, standing.

"I want to borrow your black beaded bag for the dance!" Jessica said, all animated again.

"No. No way. I'm using it that night," Elizabeth said.

"But you're wearing a green dress! It'll go *so* much

better with mine!" Jessica wheedled. "You can borrow Mom's gold clutch. I mean, I *am* going with a substandard date just to try to get you your best friend back, but if you don't even want to lend me one little bag—"

"Okay, fine." Elizabeth raised her hands in surrender. "You're right. The gold will go better with the green anyway."

"Thanks, Liz!" Jessica said, giving her a quick hug. "Okay. I'm gonna call Ronnie!"

She bounced down onto her bed and picked up her phone, shooing Elizabeth out with a wave of her hand. Elizabeth slipped out of the room and sighed. Jessica seemed pretty excited about calling a guy she supposedly wasn't even interested in. Elizabeth shook her head as she returned to the sanctuary of her own room.

If Jessica's making all the big sacrifices, Liz wondered, *then why do I suddenly feel so exhausted?*

CHAPTER
9

"WOW. THAT'S SOME story."

Roger Collins, English teacher and faculty advisor for the Oracle, leaned back in his chair and chewed on the end of his pen as he looked up at Elizabeth. With his dark blond hair, blue eyes, and perpetual tan, Mr. Collins could just as well have been an actor as a teacher. Except he didn't quite have the fashion sense down. Today he was wearing a brown plaid button-down shirt with a brown knit tie, jeans, and sneakers. Kind of like a cowboy who'd been told to dress up at the last second.

"I have to find out who told Ronnie about George

and Enid," Elizabeth said. "I just don't even know where to start."

Behind her, Olivia Davidson typed away at her Oracle computer, listening to crunchy folk music on her iPod so loud Elizabeth could actually make out the words. She was fairly confident that Olivia hadn't overheard any of the details of Enid's story. The last thing she wanted was to be blamed for anyone else's getting all the gory details. Mr. Collins, however, was different. He was a teacher. Older. Wiser. And with a keen reporter's sense. Which was why Elizabeth had finally decided to come to him for advice.

"Well. It seems to me your first step would be to figure out why someone would want to tell Ronnie about these e-mails," Mr. Collins said, sitting forward again. He folded his hands on his desk as he looked at her.

"Motivation. Right," Elizabeth said, thinking. "But motivation doesn't matter until I figure out who else could have possibly known about the letters. Otherwise I have no suspects to pin motivation on."

"Good point," Mr. Collins said with a chuckle. "So who else knew?"

"Enid says no one," Elizabeth replied, feeling as helpless as ever.

"Because *Enid* has told no one. But what about this

George guy?" Mr. Collins suggested. "Does he know anyone at SVH?"

Elizabeth's heart skipped a beat. "Winston! He knows Winston Egbert." But just as quickly, her heart dropped. "But why in the world would Winston tell Ronnie? There's nothing he could possibly gain from it, right?"

"Well, I'm sure he wouldn't have said anything to be malicious, but sometimes people tell secrets just to get attention," Mr. Collins said.

He had a point. And Winston did have kind of a big mouth sometimes. Plus he loved to be the center of attention. Practically lived for it. But he hardly knew Ronnie. He would have had to go out of his way to tell him about the letters. Which didn't really seem like something a sweet guy like Winston would do.

"I guess I could ask him," Elizabeth said.

"It's what reporters do," Mr. Collins replied with a shrug. "See what he has to say. And don't worry about Enid. She'll come around eventually. Right now she's hurting and she needs someone to blame it on. It makes sense that she'd blame it on the person closest to her."

Elizabeth stared at him, baffled. "How does that make sense?"

"Because the people we're closest to are the ones who'll forgive us for being total jerks later," he said.

Out of nowhere, Elizabeth felt all warm and happy inside. She knew she'd come to the right person.

"Oh. My. Goddess! I can not take this anymore!" Olivia pulled her earphones out and turned off her iPod, shoving away from the computer.

"What's the matter, Olivia?" Mr. Collins was on his feet, concerned.

"These letters about Ken and Ms. Dalton. I've got, like, thousands of them! My inbox is jammed," Olivia said, waving her heavily ringed hand at the screen. "I swear, we could dedicate a whole week's postings to these. If we could post obscenity."

Olivia was in charge of the opinions section on the site and always had to sift through a lot of rants about the lunches or complaints about how all the school's money went to the football team while the chess team was ignored. But lately it had been all Dalton, all the time.

"Let me see this." Mr. Collins took Olivia's mouse and opened a few of the letters, grimacing and muttering under his breath. "What is wrong with people?" he said through his teeth. "They have no idea what they're doing to her with all this. You know she's actually made herself physically ill worrying about this crap?"

Elizabeth glanced at Olivia, startled by their teacher's vehemence. Olivia pushed her brown curls off her face and

102

stood next to Liz. Another, smaller rumor that had been circulating all year was that Mr. Collins had a crush on Ms. Dalton. Now Elizabeth started to wonder if it was true.

"I heard she was even getting obscene phone calls at home," Olivia said morosely. "She had to change her number. I'd be sick too if I were her."

"The best thing to do is to ignore it," Mr. Collins said. He looked up at Olivia, his eyes sparkling with anger. "Are all the Dalton letters in this one folder?"

"Yeah," she replied.

"Good." He dragged the folder over to the recycle bin on the desktop and dumped it in. "That's what I think of those particular opinions."

"I wonder how Ken's doing. I haven't seen him in a couple of days," Elizabeth mused aloud.

"He's been out," Olivia said matter-of-factly. "I heard he has mono or something. You know, from—"

"Enough," Mr. Collins said firmly.

Olivia flinched at his tone. "Sorry, Mr. Collins."

"That's all right, Olivia. But as of this moment, I'm declaring the Oracle office a gossip-free zone," he said. "I don't want to hear any more about Ms. Dalton and Ken Matthews. The only way to stop this thing from spreading is to stop spreading it ourselves. Got it?"

"Got it," Elizabeth said as Olivia nodded mutely.

"Good. Now let's get back to work."

Mr. Collins brushed by them and Elizabeth shot Olivia a comforting glance. She knew Olivia hadn't meant to say anything wrong. It was just all anyone was talking about. It was next to impossible to ignore. And she knew from experience that it was even harder for Ms. Dalton to deal with. She knew what it was like to have conversations stop when she walked into a room. To have everyone whispering behind her back. It really could make a person sick.

Taking a deep breath, Elizabeth sat down at her own computer and opened up her folder of ideas for this week's Insider column. The first pitch was about Winston Egbert driving the wrong way down a one-way street during his driver's ed class.

Winston, Elizabeth thought. She remembered George's P.S. at the bottom of his e-mail. *Say hi to Winston for me.*

Was it possible that George and Winston were still in touch? Was there some reason that Winston would have spilled George and Enid's secret? Elizabeth was determined to find out.

• • •

"Yeah, I knew George and Enid were still e-mailing," Winston said with a shrug. "But I didn't think it was a big deal. It's not like they were having secret rendezvous or something. They're just friends."

"Exactly. There's nothing going on between them," Elizabeth said firmly.

Even though I'm sure George still likes Enid, she added to herself. She and Winston were sitting on the bleachers while football and cheerleading practices carried on in front of them. Liz had found Winston on his skateboard in the parking lot with a few friends and had basically dragged him away, not wanting to wait another second to get to the bottom of this mess.

"No. Not that I know of," Winston said, glancing up as two football helmets cracked together down on the field. "Ouch. Don't kill him, Gordo! He's on *your* team!" he shouted, earning a laugh from the cheerleading squad. Everyone except Jessica, Elizabeth noticed, who just rolled her eyes.

"Winston, I have to ask you something." Elizabeth took a deep breath. "You didn't tell Ronnie about George and Enid, did you?"

Winston's eyebrows shot up. Suddenly, she had his full attention. "Why would I do that?"

Elizabeth didn't know whether to feel relieved that her friend was innocent or upset that she was back at square one. She leaned back on the bleachers, resting her elbows on the metal bench behind her.

"I have no idea. But someone told him and he broke up with her over it, and she thinks it was me," Elizabeth said flatly.

"No way." Winston leaned back next to her, pushing his thick-rimmed glasses up on his nose. "You'd never do that."

"Glad *you* think so," Elizabeth said.

Down below, Todd ran an out route into the end zone and the backup quarterback lofted the ball right into his arms.

"Hey! Nice catch, Wilkins!" Winston shouted.

Todd looked up, then did a double take, noticing Elizabeth there for the first time. He lifted a hand in a wave. Elizabeth waved back, her heart fluttering at the attention.

"You didn't really think I went to Ronnie and told him, did you?" Winston asked, looking hurt.

"Not really, Win. I just don't know of anyone else who even knew about George," Elizabeth said with a sigh. "I thought maybe you let it slip by accident or something."

"Nope. I promised George I wouldn't tell anyone. He figured Enid would want to keep it on the DL, you know? He really is a good guy," Winston said. "He's just been through a lot."

"I can only imagine," Elizabeth said, shielding her eyes from the sun as Todd made another play. "It sounds like he really cares about Enid too."

"Totally. When you go through something like that together, I think you're pretty much bound for life," Winston said. "Those two are like that." He lifted crossed fingers, and Elizabeth noticed his knuckles were all torn up and there was a scrape on his arm, probably from some skateboarding crash. She winced but said nothing, not wanting to embarrass him. "Anyway, I know people think I'm some big blabbermouth, but I can keep my lips zipped when it counts."

Elizabeth smiled. Winston was such a good person underneath all the goofiness and the klutzy tendencies. It was too bad Jessica couldn't see it. A guy like Winston would be a much better catch than Bruce Patman, aka Mr. Conceited.

"I know you do, Win," Liz said, leaning over to give him a quick kiss on the cheek.

"Hey! Watch it, Egbert!" Todd shouted from the sidelines. His helmet was off, and he was getting some water from the huge Gatorade jug on one of the benches. "You better not be trying to snag my girl!"

Winston blushed so red he practically melded with his red SVH T-shirt. "You'll know when I'm trying to snag your girl," he replied gamely. "Right after she gives you the kiss-off!"

Elizabeth and Todd both laughed as Jessica shot her sister a disgusted look, admonishing her with one glance for even being seen with Winston. Liz rolled her eyes and smiled. Sometimes she just did not understand the way her twin's mind worked.

CHAPTER

10

"HEY. YOU DON'T look too happy for someone who's going to the dance tonight with the hottest guy on the West Coast," Todd joked, lacing his fingers with Elizabeth's on the table at Casa del Sol.

"I'm going to the dance with Jake Gyllenhaal?" Elizabeth said with mock excitement.

Todd extricated himself and held both hands over his heart, groaning. "Oh! You really know how to hit a guy where it hurts," he said with a laugh.

"Sorry. Just trying to lighten my own mood, I guess," Elizabeth said, taking a chip from their shared nacho plate and crunching into it. Outside, the breakers crashed against the rocky shore and the sun shone over the stretch of white beach farther down along the water. Another gorgeous Sweet Valley day. Elizabeth wanted to be excited about the dance, but she just couldn't stop thinking about Enid. Yesterday after school she had attempted to corner her friend at home, but Enid wouldn't even come to the door.

"Liz, you've done everything you can," Todd said, his tone suddenly serious. Elizabeth looked at him, touched that he knew exactly what she was thinking. "You have to try to let it go. Hope that eventually she'll figure it out."

"It just doesn't make any sense," Elizabeth said, slumping slightly in the orange vinyl booth. "Enid was the only one who believed me when the whole Rick Andover thing happened—"

Todd winced. "Have I mentioned how sorry I am about that?"

Elizabeth smiled. "About ten thousand times. But my point is, she trusted me then. Why can't she trust me now? What's different this time?"

"What's different is, she's the one that's hurt," Todd said with a shrug. "She's not thinking straight."

"You sound like Mr. Collins," Elizabeth teased.

Todd considered this, shoving a chili-laden chip into his mouth. "I guess there are worse people to sound like. Anyway, if Enid's really your friend, she'll come around."

"*Exactly* like Mr. Collins," Elizabeth said.

"Well, he's feeding me my lines," Todd joked. "I have an earpiece in right now. It's all very *24*."

"Ha ha," Elizabeth said, reaching for her ice water. "As long as Jessica's not talking in your ear. She says I'm better off without Enid."

Todd pulled a face and straightened up in his seat. "Yeah, I wouldn't exactly listen to your sister when it comes to friendship."

Todd was still bitter over the fact that Jessica had manipulated him into thinking that Elizabeth didn't want to go out with him—and vice versa. After all the lies Jessica had spewed trying to keep the two of them apart, Todd trusted Jessica about as far as he could kick her. Elizabeth, meanwhile, had forgiven Jessica. Just like she always had. Just like she always would. When it came down to it, they would always be sisters. And over the years, Jessica had done as much to help Elizabeth as she'd done to hurt her.

I think, Elizabeth said to herself.

"Jessica means well," Elizabeth told Todd. "I mean, who could blame her for wanting you?"

Todd's eyes sparkled. He tilted his head in a cocky way. "True. She does have good taste."

Elizabeth laughed and took another chip. "But seriously, I think she really does want to help this time. I mean, do you really think she wants me to lose my best friend?"

"I don't know what she wants," Todd said, sipping his drink. "That girl is an enigma."

"Nice use of an SAT word!" Elizabeth congratulated him.

"Caught that, did ya?" Todd replied. "I just think you should trust your own gut about Enid. Not Jessica's."

"I'm not sure I can trust my gut anymore," Elizabeth said. "This thing has me so mixed up I can hardly see straight."

"Well, as long as you can see straight long enough to make it to my car tonight, I'm good," Todd said. He took her hand again and kissed her palm quickly. "Come on, Liz. Just try to let it go for one night and have a good time."

"I just wish I didn't feel so guilty," Elizabeth said. "As far as I know, Enid's staying home tonight. She's nominated for homecoming queen and she's not even going to be there! How am I supposed to have fun when she's sitting at home all sad and stuff?"

Todd smiled. He got up and went around to her side of the booth, wrapping her in his strong arms.

"You are too sweet," he said, kissing her cheek.

"Sweet and depressed," she said mopily.

"Well, luckily, I have a thing for depressed blondes," Todd joked.

"Todd!"

Elizabeth looked at him out of the corner of her eye and her heart flip-flopped. Todd leaned in to kiss her, and just like that, everything else faded away—the piped-in Spanish music, the waves crashing outside, and all thoughts of Enid. Whenever Todd kissed her, all Elizabeth could think about was being in his arms forever.

● ● ●

"Jess! What are you doing?" Elizabeth asked as she walked into her room. "Mom said you can't go to the dance until your room is clean!"

Jessica looked up from Elizabeth's computer. She was wearing an SVU T-shirt of their brother's and a pair of Elizabeth's shorts. Sometimes Elizabeth wondered if Jessica even knew she had about four wardrobes' worth of her own clothes strewn all over the floor of her bedroom.

"Sorry! God! Lila just sent me a picture of her dress," Jessica said, standing. "Have a heart attack, why don't you?"

Elizabeth sighed. "I'm just trying to help you, Jess. You only have an hour."

"Well, if you really want to help me, then come help

me," Jessica said, lifting her hands and letting them slap down against her thighs. "I mean, the place looks like a hurricane zone. I don't know how I'm supposed to do it alone in one hour."

Maybe you should have started three days ago, when Mom laid down the law, Elizabeth thought.

"Fine. I'll be there in a minute," Elizabeth said. "I just want to check my e-mail."

"Cool. Thanks, Lizzie!"

Jessica bounded out of the room, and seconds later her stereo was booming again. Elizabeth sat down at her computer. Jessica's e-mail screen was still up, and she hadn't bothered to log out, of course. Elizabeth was about to log out for her when something caught her eye. It was an e-mail from Ronnie, dated two weeks ago. The subject line read "RE: thought you should know . . ."

Elizabeth's heart started to pound like crazy. Two weeks ago Enid and Ronnie were still together. There was no reason for Jessica and Ronnie to be e-mailing each other. Glancing over her shoulder, Elizabeth hovered the cursor over the message. She knew she shouldn't, but her gut was telling her she should. And what had Todd just said? Trust her gut . . .

She clicked the message open.

Jessica,
I don't believe this. Thanks for letting
me know.
Ronnie

Below his message was the message Jessica had sent to him. The message he had replied to. And there were five documents attached to it. Elizabeth recognized the attachments instantly. They were Enid's code for naming her messages to and from George: his initials, and the dates of the e-mails. "GW711." "GW613." Jessica had sent five of George and Enid's e-mails to Ronnie.

Elizabeth suddenly felt so sick she was light-headed. Her fingers shook as she closed the browser. Right in the center of her desktop, Enid's folder of e-mails glowed like a reprimand. She should have put it right in the recycle bin. She should never have left it there for anyone to see.

No. Not just anyone. Jessica.

This is not your fault, Elizabeth told herself, clenching her teeth. *It's hers. All hers. How could you ever imagine that she would* do *something like this?*

Elizabeth took a deep breath, trying to calm her rising fury. All this time Jessica had been pretending to try to help her. Pretending that she wanted Enid and Ronnie back together and that she wanted Enid to forgive

Elizabeth. Meanwhile, it was all her fault that any of it had happened in the first place. Todd was right. Trusting Jessica was a mistake. A huge, *huge* mistake.

"Liz! I thought you were going to come help me!" Jessica shouted from her room.

Elizabeth got up, walked over to her bedroom door and glared across the hall at her sister. Jessica stood in her own doorway wearing an indignant expression. Elizabeth wanted to lunge across the hall and strangle her. But she couldn't. Not this way. Her revenge for this one was going to be much bigger than that.

"Yeah, well, I changed my mind," she told Jessica.

Then she slammed the door right in her sister's stunned face.

CHAPTER

11

ENID STARED THROUGH the glass doors in the freezer section of the supermarket, trying to decide if buying three pints of ice cream on a Saturday night would make her irrevocably pathetic. The problem was, the supermarket just happened to have all three of her favorite Ben & Jerry's flavors in stock. First time that had ever happened. It was like the ice cream gods were telling her she *should* stay home from the dance, and this was their way of keeping her company.

"Screw it," Enid said under her breath.

She yanked the door open, grabbed the three pints, and tucked them under her arm. When she turned around to make a beeline for the express lane, she stopped in her tracks. Ms. Dalton was standing two freezer doors away, staring at the Häagen-Dazs. It took Enid a second to recognize her in her Dodgers baseball cap and sunglasses, but it was definitely her. And it looked as if she was on the same drown-her-sorrows mission Enid was on. Enid was just trying to decide whether to say something or pretend she hadn't seen her when Ms. Dalton looked up and did a double take.

"Enid! Hello. I didn't see you there." Ms. Dalton reached back to touch her ponytail nervously.

"Hi, Ms. Dalton," Enid said, feeling awkward.

The teacher's eyes darted to Enid's contraband. "Planning a night in, I see."

Enid's face flushed. "Homecoming doesn't exactly appeal to me today."

"Why not? Aren't you nominated for queen?" the teacher asked, incredulous.

Enid's bottom lip started to quiver and she felt like an idiot. But this was how it had been lately. The tears came out of nowhere, and at the most irritating and embarrassing moments.

"Oh, I'm so sorry! Did I say something wrong?" Ms. Dalton asked.

"No! I'm just—"

Enid covered her face with her free hand and Ms. Dalton hurried over. She took the ice cream from the crook of Enid's arm and replaced it in the freezer, then wrapped her arm around Enid's shoulders.

"Come on. We're going to get some coffee," she said, giving Enid a light squeeze.

"Okay," Enid half whimpered.

Ms. Dalton led her to the back of the sprawling market, where there was a small coffee bar next to the bakery. She ordered a pair of iced coffees, then sat down at the tiny, tile-topped table where Enid had already hunkered down. Removing her cap and sunglasses, Ms. Dalton cleared her throat and focused on Enid.

"Tell me what's going on," she said.

So Enid did. She told her the whole sordid story from start to finish. And by the time she was done, she was sitting up straight again and the tears were gone. It was the first time she had told someone everything that had happened, and she felt ten times lighter just from the telling.

"Wow," Ms. Dalton said. She took a sip of her coffee and raised her eyebrows. "That's a lot to handle in a couple of weeks."

"Tell me about it," Enid said.

"It's tough being convicted without a trial, isn't it?" Ms. Dalton mused aloud.

Something in her tone made a pang strike Enid's heart. She looked at her teacher again—her pale face, her red-rimmed eyes. The woman hadn't even been in school for three days, thanks to all the nasty rumors flying around.

"Omigosh. I'm such an idiot," Enid said. "Like you really want to listen to this right now."

"Enid, please. Do not worry about it." Ms. Dalton leaned forward in her chair. "It's actually kind of nice to focus on something other than my own problems. Not that I'm happy this happened to you, but . . ."

Enid smiled sympathetically. "I know what you mean." She took a deep breath and pushed her hair back from her face, all business. "Okay. So what should I do?"

"Well, first of all, you should hear Elizabeth out," Ms. Dalton said.

"What?" Enid asked, shocked. The very thought of Elizabeth and her backstabbing made her stomach squirm.

"I know this is tough to hear, but by not giving her a chance to explain, you're basically doing the same thing to her that Ronnie did to you when the two of you broke up," Ms. Dalton said, looking Enid in the eye.

Now Enid really did squirm. "I never thought of it that way."

"Well, you've been angry," Ms. Dalton said with a forgiving look. "People miss a lot of stuff when they're angry. Just talk to her. I'm sure Liz will understand."

Enid took a deep breath. After all the times she'd hung up on Liz and refused to talk to her, the idea of approaching her friend was hugely intimidating. What if Elizabeth had already decided to write her off? She shuddered and decided to focus on the second part of her problem.

"Okay, but what about the dance?" she asked. "I never thought in a million years I'd get nominated for homecoming queen. And I have this incredible dress . . ."

"So go by yourself," Ms. Dalton said. Like it was the most obvious and simple thing in the world.

Enid snorted a laugh and took a big gulp of her coffee. "Yeah, right."

"Why not? You don't need a man at your side to go to some little dance," Ms. Dalton said, getting fired up by her own pep talk. "You're a young, beautiful, confident woman. I say you go in there, hold your head high, and make Ronnie Edwards eat his heart out."

"I heard he's going to the dance with Jessica Wakefield. He won't even notice I'm there," Enid said wryly, her chest constricting.

"Eh, that girl's all cookie-cutter flash," Ms. Dalton

said with a wave of her hand. "You, my dear, are a time-less beauty."

"You're insane," Enid said, blushing hard as she laughed.

"Yes, but in a good way," Ms. Dalton said, her eyes sparkling for the first time in days. Enid's heart warmed to see her favorite teacher looking somewhat like herself again.

"Ms. Dalton, I just want you to know that I don't believe any of that stuff they're saying about you," Enid said impulsively.

"Thanks, Enid," Ms. Dalton said, looking down at the table. "That means a lot. Especially since I've pretty much decided to resign."

Enid felt as if the floor had just tilted beneath her. "What? No!"

"Well, there's been a lot of pressure from the school board," Ms. Dalton said, looking grim. "No one wants to see SVH and a story like this on the front page."

"But there's no story!" Enid protested, gripping the sides of the table. "It's not true!"

"That doesn't matter to them," Ms. Dalton said, the spark completely gone now.

"No. You can't just give up." Enid was fuming. "What about all that stuff you just said about being a strong, confident woman? About holding my head high? How am I supposed to do that when you won't even stand up for yourself?"

"Enid, it's not the same thing," Ms. Dalton said.

"Fine. Whatever," Enid said, standing. She grabbed her messenger bag and shoved the strap up on her shoulder. "But I think it is. We were both accused of something we didn't do, right? So what's the difference?"

Ms. Dalton looked desperate and sad and pale. "Enid—"

"Forget it. I have to go," Enid said, turning on her heel.

As she shoved through the front door of the supermarket, her teeth were clenched together in anger. How many people she cared about were going to disappoint her?

• • •

"You look incredible. And you're going to have an incredible time," Enid told herself, gazing at her reflection in the mirror. Her eyes were lined, her lashes curled, her blush applied, her new lip gloss in place. Everything was perfect. Except for the fact that Ronnie was on the other side of town picking up Jessica right now. Enid watched her face crumple. "Or you'll just walk in, see Jessica and Ronnie dancing together, and run out of there in tears like a big fat loser," she muttered.

With a sigh, Enid turned around and shoved her lip gloss into her black clutch purse. She didn't even know why she had decided to go to the dance. Just to show Ms. Dalton that she could do what the teacher herself couldn't do? To show Ronnie he hadn't affected her? To see if she had the slimmest of shots at being crowned homecoming queen? Now that she was standing there in her room with nothing left to do but walk out the door, none of those inducements seemed all that compelling. She glanced at her bed and the remote for her TV. Now, *that* looked compelling. . . .

The doorbell rang and Enid jumped. Her heart went so ballistic it was as if a bomb had gone off.

"Okay. Chill," she told herself, smoothing the front of her silky black dress. Maybe she shouldn't have had that iced coffee with Ms. Dalton. It seemed to be making her even more tense than she already was.

"Enid!" her mother called up the stairs. "There's someone here to see you!"

"Who?" Enid called. The last person who had stopped by unexpectedly was Elizabeth, but she had to be getting ready for the dance herself now. Who else could it possibly . . .

Ronnie!

Enid's heart leapt. Maybe he had changed his mind!

Maybe he had decided to take her to the dance after all! Enid checked her face one last time and flew out of her bedroom, racing down the stairs in her bare feet. She saw her mother's face first, and it was shining with mischief. Enid was just wondering what that was all about when she looked up and her breath caught in her throat.

"George!" she gasped.

George Warren had gotten hot. The semiskinny, borderline dorky kid who had left the Valley was gone, and in his place was a tall, broad, blond and green-eyed Abercrombie model. He was wearing a black pin-striped suit and filling it out *very* well. The moment he laid eyes on Enid, his whole face lit up with a smile that could have caused every girl within a hundred-mile radius to swoon.

"Sorry for the surprise visit," George said. "I tried your cell, but it kept going right to voice mail."

Even his voice had changed. It had a deep, rumbling quality that made Enid's knees buckle. She clung to the banister. How was this possible? How was it that after all this time he could still have that effect on her? She had thought they were just friends, but according to her spasming heart, she'd been very, *very* wrong.

"Yeah, I've been . . . keeping it turned off," Enid said breathlessly. *The better to avoid Liz's calls.*

"I'll leave you two alone," Mrs. Rollins said with a smile. "It was good to see you, George."

"You too, Mrs. Rollins," George said.

Enid's mother winked at her as she walked by on her way to the kitchen. Enid had to bite her tongue to keep from laughing. She and George just stared at each other for a long moment. Enid's heart was pounding wildly, and she was almost afraid to speak, certain she would say something totally stupid and embarrassing.

"So, you've changed," George said finally.

"Look who's talking!" Enid replied with a laugh.

"You lost the bangs," George said, looking admiringly at her hair as he stepped closer to her. "And the braces."

"And you got muscles!" Enid exclaimed, reaching for his arm. Yep. Serious biceps under there.

George laughed. "Man. It's good to see you. I mean, I knew it would be, but I didn't know *how* good."

"It's good to see you too," Enid said, smiling.

George reached out and pulled her into a big, warm hug. Enid pressed her cheek to his chest and sighed, taking in the clean, freshly shaven scent of him. She could hardly believe he was here, that this was happening—that he was so drop-dead gorgeous.

"So listen, Winston kind of filled me in on what's been going on," George said, pulling back. His green eyes were suddenly serious as they searched her face. "I'm so sorry about the e-mails. I never thought they'd cause World War Three."

Enid chuckled. Suddenly, Ronnie seemed very far away. "It wasn't exactly World War Three."

"It's just that . . . you should know that talking to you . . . even on e-mail . . . that was really the only thing that kept me going at first," George said. "You have no idea how many times I wanted to give up those first few months, but then I'd get an e-mail from you and . . ." George smiled again and put his hands in his pockets. "You were really there for me, Enid. And I just wanted to say thanks."

Enid was completely floored. She had never imagined that her silly notes and encouragements would have such an impact. "You're welcome, I guess," she said with a shrug.

"I just hate to think that *those* e-mails got you in trouble," George said.

"Don't worry about it. Really," Enid told him.

"Well, I was hoping to make it up to you," George said with a mischievous smile. He turned and picked up a plastic box from the table near the door. In all the shock, Enid hadn't noticed it. George opened it up and removed a white orchid corsage from inside.

"Enid Rollins, will you go to homecoming with me?" he asked with a hopeful expression, holding out the orchid.

"Are you kidding me? Of course!" she replied.

George broke into a wide grin and Enid threw her arms around his neck. He held her tightly for a moment, and when he pulled back, his cheek brushed hers. A sizzle of attraction shot right through Enid. They looked into each other's eyes, but then Enid quickly looked away. There was no way a guy this beautiful could actually want to kiss her.

"Okay, so I guess we should go," she said, taking the orchid and snapping the band around her wrist. She turned and headed for the door.

"Uh, Enid? Haven't you forgotten something?" George asked, his eyes laughing as he looked down at her feet.

Enid suddenly realized her toes were rather cold. "My shoes!"

"Don't worry about it. Barefoot girls are less likely to run away," George joked. "I've seen statistics."

"Why would I want to run away?" Enid asked.

"Oh, I don't know. In case I tried to do this," George said.

He grabbed her wrist, pulled her to him, and leaned in for a gentle, tentative kiss. Enid's heart stopped completely as he cupped the sides of her face with his strong hands. He looked at her, heavy-lidded, a question in his eyes—asking if this was okay.

"Like I said. Why would I want to run away?" Enid asked again, her voice a whisper.

George smiled his heart-stopping smile. His next kiss was a lot less tentative. In fact, it was completely and totally perfect.

CHAPTER
12

"WELL? HOW DO I look?"

Jessica struck a sexy pose—arm up, hip out—in the doorway of Elizabeth's bedroom. Her slinky red dress was stunning, and looked perfect with the black strappy heels and Elizabeth's beaded bag.

Like the devil, Elizabeth thought, taking a deep breath as she smoothed her hair back.

"You look like you just stepped out of *Maxim* magazine," Elizabeth said curtly. She turned to the side to check that the fuller skirt of her green dress was wrinkle free. "Are you sure Ronnie can handle it?"

Jessica rolled her eyes and stepped over to the smaller

mirror above the dresser, checking her face. "It's not like I'm gonna hook up with him, Liz. I told you. I'm only going with him for Enid."

"Uh-huh. You did tell me something like that," Elizabeth said sarcastically, plucking her gold earrings off her dresser. She pushed them into her ears, wishing she could stab something much sharper into Jessica's head.

"Okay, Liz. What's up with you?" Jessica asked, turning to her with her hand on her hip. "First you throw that tantrum and don't help me with my room, and now you're being all snippy. What's going on?"

"Nothing," Elizabeth said with a shrug. "Nothing at all."

She picked up her cell and checked for messages. Not a one. She had left a rambling message on Enid's phone over an hour ago, telling her all about Jessica's involvement and begging her to call back. But still, nothing. Was Enid never going to forgive her?

"Then why do you keep looking at me like you're a fat chick and I'm a plate of evil carbs?" Jessica asked, lifting a hand. "Are you mad at me for something?"

"Mad? Why would I be mad?" Elizabeth asked sweetly. She tossed her phone into her mother's gold clutch. "Maybe it's all in your head. Do you have a guilty conscience about something?"

Jessica frowned. She flicked her hair over her shoulder

with her freshly polished nails. *"No,"* she said firmly. "It's not like I've done anything wrong."

"In that case, you have nothing to worry about," Elizabeth said with a blithe shrug.

"You are so irritating sometimes, you know that?" Jessica said with a groan. "I mean, God! I'm trying to do something nice for *your* friend and you're not even thanking me for it."

"That is so not true!" Elizabeth replied, dropping some cash into the bag as well. "I'm just trying to think of a good way to show my appreciation for everything you've done."

"You are?" Jessica's expression brightened.

Elizabeth narrowed her beautiful blue-green eyes. "Of course. I want to see you get everything you deserve, Jess," she said, patting her sister on her tanned shoulder.

"Thanks, Liz. I knew you couldn't be completely oblivious," Jessica said with a smile.

Oh, no. I'm not the one who's oblivious, Elizabeth thought, barely keeping her anger in check.

"So what do you think?" Jessica said, turning to her reflection again. "Should I wear my hair up or down?"

"Better leave it down. If you do an updo they might not know how to place the crown," Liz said.

"Omigosh! You're so right!" Jessica exclaimed. "Why didn't I think of that?" She grabbed Elizabeth's brush and quickly ran it through her hair until it gleamed. "Do you really think I'll win?"

"Don't you always get what you want?" Elizabeth asked wryly.

"Well, if I do, don't be too disappointed. At least you were still nominated," Jessica said, turning her face from side to side. "But oh my God, if I do win, and Bruce wins, then we're going to do the spotlight dance together! He is going to *die* when he sees me in this dress. I just know it!"

"Don't get too excited. There's no guaranteeing he'll win," Elizabeth said.

"Oh, please. He's Bruce Patman," Jessica responded with a guffaw. "Todd and Ken are totally going to split the jock vote, and *no one's* going to vote for Winston Egbert."

Elizabeth grabbed her digital camera and sauntered out the door to wait for Todd in the foyer. On her way out, she cast Jessica a sly look that Jessica completely missed. She was too busy practicing her surprised reaction in the mirror.

"I don't know, Jess," Elizabeth said. "I happen to think Winston would make some lucky girl a fantastic king."

● ● ●

"Wow, Ronnie. This is incredible," Elizabeth said as they walked into the gym. "You did a great job."

"Thanks, Liz," Ronnie said, looking at his feet with chagrin.

See? I can be nice. Even though you shattered my best friend's heart, I can be as sweet as apple pie, Elizabeth thought.

She looked around the gym, which was already packed with couples dancing to the DJ's driving beat. Every inch of space was covered with the SVH red and white, from the thick swags of fabric draping the ceiling, to the balloons all over the floor, to the huge posters of athletes and students that adorned the walls.

"Yeah, if people don't leave here with school spirit, they'll never get it," Todd said, pulling Elizabeth closer to his side.

"When does the voting start?" Jessica asked. "I can't wait!"

"Me neither," Elizabeth said flatly. She glanced around and quickly spotted Caroline Pearce over by the snack table. She was hard to miss in her hot pink dress with her red hair done in a thousand tight ringlets.

"I'm going to go grab something to eat. I barely had dinner. Anyone want anything?" Elizabeth asked, pointing.

"No. I'm good!" Jessica trilled happily.

"I'll come with you," Todd offered.

Elizabeth smiled and took his hand as they crossed the room. He looked as handsome as ever in his blue suit and light blue tie. Most of the guys in the room could hardly pull off their outfits, looking as though they were playing dress-up in their fathers' clothes as they tugged at their collars or pulled at their sleeves. But Todd, well, he could wear anything and look totally comfortable.

"Some spread," Todd said, eyeing the table of cookies and sandwiches and salty snacks. "What's your pleasure?"

"Just grab me a few cookies and some punch, okay?" Elizabeth said, touching his arm. "I have to talk to Caroline real quick. I'll be right back."

"You got it," Todd said.

Before she'd even gotten two steps away he was already loading up on sweets. Elizabeth grabbed Caroline's wrist and Caroline stopped midgab. She eyed Liz with consternation at first, until Elizabeth leaned in and whispered in her ear. Then her green eyes widened in delight.

"Crazy, huh?" Elizabeth said, grinning.

"Totally," Caroline agreed.

Liz turned and strode back to Todd, knowing her mission was accomplished. When Caroline Pearce and her mouth were involved, there was no way she could lose.

● ● ●

"Having fun?" Todd asked, touching his forehead to Elizabeth's as they swayed back and forth on the dance floor to a slow tune.

"So far, so perfect," she replied, squeezing his hand.

He was just about to touch his lips to hers when a commotion by the door caught their attention. Ms. Dalton had just walked in wearing a gorgeous deep egg-plant dress, her hair back in a sleek twist. Everyone was whispering as she walked by, but she kept her head up and pretended nothing was amiss.

"I wondered if she was going to show," Todd said. "She's been out all week."

"Good for her," Elizabeth put in.

"Hey, Ms. Dalton! Where's Ken?" someone shouted.

There was a general gasp and Ms. Dalton hesitated a brief second before continuing right on over to the re-freshment table, where the other chaperones were gath-ered. Mr. Collins greeted her with a warm smile and placed his hand on her back, bending his head close to hers. He whispered something in her ear and Ms. Dalton laughed. The other parents and teachers shook her hand in a welcoming way.

"Looks like she's doing better," Elizabeth said, sighing in relief.

"People are still going to talk," Todd said as they started dancing again.

"They'll get tired of it after a while and move on to something else," Elizabeth predicted. She'd seen it happen a thousand times, after all.

"Let's just hope it's not us," Todd joked.

"What could we possibly give them to talk about?" Elizabeth asked, shaking her hair down her back as she looked up at him. "We're way too boring."

Todd feigned shock. "I'll give you boring."

He leaned in and tickled the spot just behind Elizabeth's ear with his lips. She practically melted into him.

"Okay! Okay! We're not boring!" she giggled, shoving him back.

"Thank you," Todd said with a nod.

Elizabeth shook her head. Her eyes fell on Lila, standing alone in her sleek blue dress, over by the door.

"Hey. So where *is* Ken, anyway?" Elizabeth whispered. "I thought he was coming with Lila."

"Yeah, right. After he found out she was the one who started the Dalton rumor and e-mailed that ridiculous picture to everyone?" Todd said incredulously.

"That was *her*?" Elizabeth asked, her jaw dropping.

"You didn't hear this?" Todd asked. "Wow. I can't believe I know something before the Insider does. Hang on. I need a minute to bask in my pride."

Elizabeth whacked his shoulder. "Shut up! Why would she do something like that that?"

"Ken asked her and she finally admitted she wanted to break up Dalton and her dad," Todd said. "When the rumors alone weren't doing their job, she came up with the picture idea. So she took that picture of Ms. Dalton when she was licking her lips of whipped cream at some party she was at with her dad, then found some random picture of Ken. One quick Photoshop session and the job was done."

"Oh my God. She's an evil genius. After the picture hit they were both out of school for days, which just made the rumor get bigger and bigger," Liz said.

"Pretty much," Todd replied.

"Wow. Ken must have loved being sucked into that particular drama," Liz commented.

"Not so much. Which is why he's not here," Todd said.

"Ken Matthews skipping homecoming," Elizabeth said, shaking her head. "It just doesn't seem right."

"He'll be at the after party, believe me," Todd said with a smirk. "He just wanted to show Lila she couldn't just mess with people's lives like that."

Elizabeth glanced at Lila, who sighed morosely and checked her watch. Lesson learned, apparently. Then Jessica joined her friend and they started talking urgently. Elizabeth's stomach turned at the very sight of her conniving sister.

Lila's not the only one who's going to learn a lesson tonight, Elizabeth thought. *Hope you're ready for that crown, Jess . . .*

● ● ●

Elizabeth was standing near the wall when the single hottest guy she had ever seen besides Todd Wilkins stepped through the doors of the gym. Her heart actually skipped a beat at the sight of him, and she was glad Todd was over at the punch bowl in case her reaction was obvious on her face. But when she saw who Gorgeous Guy's date was, her heart *really* stopped.

"Enid!" Elizabeth gasped before she could check herself.

Enid turned and looked at Liz. For the first time in over a week there was color in Enid's cheeks and her eyes were bright and happy. Elizabeth waited for all that to change when Enid saw her, but it didn't. Instead, Enid whispered something to her mystery date, then strode right over and hugged Elizabeth. Almost squeezed the breath out of her.

"Liz! I am *so* sorry! I just got your message! I haven't had my phone on for days, but I just listened to it in the car," Enid rambled. "I can't believe I was so mad at you!"

"It's okay," Elizabeth said, still a bit stunned by the

hug. "I'm so glad you got it. I was worried you weren't coming and I wouldn't get to explain . . ."

"I feel like such an idiot. I can't believe I ever thought you would do that to me. It was just . . . there was no one else, and—"

"I know, Enid. Believe me. Even I couldn't figure out who else there was to blame," Elizabeth said.

"If I were you I would hate me right now," Enid said, shaking her head. "How could we not have thought of Jessica?"

"I have no idea," Elizabeth replied. "I think she has some kind of mind meld on all of us. Especially me. It's like every time she does something horrible I think it's a fluke and forget about it."

"Do you think she's a witch?" Enid joked.

"Maybe," Elizabeth mused aloud. "But don't worry. I have a plan for her."

"A burning at the stake, maybe?" Enid asked.

"Not exactly. But to her it'll be close," Elizabeth said, narrowing her eyes. "So you're not mad?"

"Please. I'm totally over it," Enid said with a wave of her hand. "Actually, Jessica kind of did me a favor," she added, lowering her voice. She glanced over at her hot date and smiled. He was standing a safe distance away, pretending to be enthralled by the decorations. "George!" Enid shouted to be heard over the music.

"George?" Elizabeth whispered, shocked.

"Uh-huh," Enid replied with a grin. He stepped over, his hands behind his back, and smiled. "George Warren, this is my best friend, Elizabeth Wakefield."

"Nice to meet you," George said.

"You too," Elizabeth replied, grinning.

"Mind if I steal her?" George asked, taking Enid's hand. "I love this song."

"No! Please! Steal away," Elizabeth said, raising her hands.

George smiled and turned toward the dance floor, but Enid turned back to whisper to Liz. "See? Big favor!"

Elizabeth laughed. "I got it."

She took a deep breath and smiled after her friend as she and George made their way to the center of the dance floor. Liz was happy that her friend seemed to be genuinely psyched about George, but she couldn't forget all the misery she and Enid had been through for the past couple of weeks. Even if Jessica *had* done Enid a big favor, she hadn't meant to. She had *meant* to make everyone unhappy, just so she could have her way.

As Enid and George got cozy under the twinkling lights, Elizabeth noticed a number of people staring at them. Enid looked so sophisticated in her black dress, and George was causing several girls to drool. Elizabeth scanned the room for Jessica and Ronnie and found them a few feet away from Enid. They had stopped dancing and both were gaping at Enid and her date. Jessica appeared dumbfounded, while Ronnie looked simply murderous.

Elizabeth giggled under her breath. Enid and George hadn't been part of her little revenge plan, but they'd sure gotten the night started off right.

"Attention, everyone! Can I have your attention, please!" Ms. Dalton's voice cut through the air. "You have five more minutes to vote for homecoming king and queen! Five more minutes and then the other chaperones and I are off to tally the votes. Make sure your voice is heard!"

A few stragglers hustled over to the voting table, and Elizabeth smiled as she saw Caroline and Cara whispering nearby.

I have a feeling my voice has already been heard, she thought. *Loud and clear.*

CHAPTER
13

A BREATHLESS HUSH fell over the gymnasium as Ronnie Edwards took the stage to announce the results of the homecoming vote. Free of her date for the first time all night, Jessica casually sidled up next to Bruce Patman and his date, who were standing near the back wall. Bruce looked beyond handsome in his casual yet expensive suit. He'd gone tieless, as if to say he was too good for this dressing-up-for-school-dances crap, and he smelled delicious. Jessica flicked her eyes over the trust-fund baby on his arm. Her hair had been dyed one too many times, and her skin was way too oily. Bruce deserved so much better.

"Good luck, Bruce," Jessica said quietly.

"You too, Wakefield," he said, glancing down at her. He smiled sexily. "Like you need it."

Jessica's heart fluttered. There he went again, making her feel like she was the only girl in the room. Next he would turn around and blow her off. But not this time. Not if she had anything to say about it. She glanced at Enid, who stood chatting happily with her random hot date. Jessica had a feeling that even though Enid had shown up, she had edged her out in the vote. Most people had already cast their ballots before Enid had deigned to walk through the door.

I have to win. I just have to. If I have to watch Enid Rollins dancing with Bruce Patman, I will just die.

"All right, everyone. This is the moment we've all been waiting for," Ronnie said into the microphone. He didn't sound very excited himself. In fact, his voice was a dead monotone.

Okay, Mr. Boring. Get on with it, Jessica thought. The gym was completely silent.

"This year's Sweet Valley High homecoming queen is . . ."

Jessica Wakefield, Jessica Wakefield, Jessica Wakefield.

"Jessica Wakefield!" Ronnie announced.

"Omigod!" Jessica trilled, bringing both hands to cover her mouth. "I don't believe it!"

The gym erupted in applause. Jessica turned her big blue-green eyes up to look at Bruce. "See you up there in a minute," she said slyly.

Bruce grinned in response. As Jessica made her way through the crowd, a few of her friends hugged her, and everyone was shouting their congratulations. She climbed the steps to the makeshift stage and shook her hair back. Mr. Collins lifted the sparkling rhinestone crown and she dipped slightly to accept it. When she felt the weight of it on her head, she felt as if all her dreams were coming true. She faced the crowd, grinning uncontrollably. She was homecoming queen. She *was* the most popular girl in school. And any second now, she'd be joined onstage by Bruce Patman and they'd be dancing together under the spotlight. It didn't get more perfect than this.

"Okay, quiet down now. Quiet down," Ronnie said into the microphone, sounding like a scolding father. Jessica shot him a look. Why did he have to be so blah? Maybe he and Enid *had* been better off together. "And now for our homecoming king. This was a landslide victory, people. Your Sweet Valley High homecoming king is . . ."

Bruce Patman! Jessica thought, giddy.

"Winston Egbert!" Ronnie announced.

"What?" Jessica blurted out.

There was a loud whoop from the back of the gym and everyone laughed. As Winston practically skipped toward the stage, the cheers that followed him were even louder than Jessica's had been. Her jaw dropped as Winston appeared in a hideous gray suit and bounded up the stairs toward her. One step from the stage, he tripped over the lip and went sprawling on the floor right at her feet. Everyone stopped clapping. Winston looked up.

"My queen," he joked.

Laughter echoed all around. Jessica grimaced. This was not happening. This was so not happening. She looked out at the crowd, trying to catch a glimpse of Bruce, but he'd been swallowed up by all the well-wishers gunning for the stage to congratulate Winston. He finally scrambled to his feet and accepted the crown.

"Ladies and gentlemen! Your king and queen!" Ronnie announced, stepping back.

Winston reached for Jessica's hand and thrust it in the air as if they'd just won some boxing match. A thousand flashbulbs went off, searing thousands of tiny dots into Jessica's vision. She wrenched her arm away and touched her crown. This couldn't be real. All those dreams. All those visions of her pressed up against Bruce, dancing with him in front of the whole school. She had never wanted anything so badly in her life. And now she was going to be dancing with *Winston*?

"Jess! Jess! Congratulations!" Cara shouted in front of the stage.

Jessica turned away from Winston and stormed down the steps. "What do you mean 'congratulations'?" she said through her teeth. "How the hell did Winston win this thing? Is this a joke? There's no way he could have beaten out Bruce!"

"Wait a minute. . . . I thought you wanted Winston to win," Cara said, her brow creasing in confusion.

On the stage, Winston took the microphone to make a speech. Everyone was cheering and laughing and rolling their eyes.

"What? Why the hell would I want that?" Jessica asked.

"Well, that's what everyone's been saying. That you've got some huge crush on him and you wanted you guys to be king and queen," Cara explained. "I thought it was a little weird since you've been talking about nothing but Bruce, but I just figured you'd moved on. As always."

"As always?" Jessica sputtered. "Cara! Even if I do change my mind about guys *once in a while*, I would never, *ever* have a crush on Winston Egbert! I'd have to be insane from freaking malaria or something!"

"Oh." Cara bit her lip and shrugged. "Sorry, Jess. Guess I shouldn't have told so many people about it!"

Jessica screeched in frustration and brought her hands to her head. "Who would start such a stupid rumor?" she demanded. "Why would anyone want to torture me so badly? I just can't—"

And then it hit her. Elizabeth's cool demeanor before the dance. Her comment about how Winston would make some lucky girl a great king. But why? Why the hell would Elizabeth do something like this? Jessica turned around, her anger fuming out of control, and nearly walked right into her twin.

"Jessica! Congratulations!" Elizabeth trilled, throwing her arms around her sister. "I knew you were going to win!"

"Liz. How could you do this to me?" Jessica said, her jaw clenched. "How could you set it up so that I'd have to dance with Winston Egbert? What the hell did I ever do to you?"

Elizabeth's jaw dropped. She looked right into Jessica's miserable face and laughed. Jessica's hands curled into fists, ready to punch her sister right then and there.

"What did *you* ever do to *me*?" Elizabeth pondered aloud. "Well, let's see. You looked at my private files on my computer. You e-mailed all Enid's biggest secrets to her boyfriend and got him to break up with her. You then let her blame it all on me, told me you were going to fix it, and instead did everything you could to make it worse. Let's see. Have I left anything out?"

Jessica was stunned. How on earth had Elizabeth figured all that out? "I—"

"Don't even bother trying to explain," Elizabeth said. "I know all you wanted was that crown. Well, you've got it now, sis. Live it up."

"And now, would the king and queen please take the floor for their spotlight dance?" Mr. Collins announced. Everyone cheered. Slowly, Winston descended the stairs, keeping his chin up and feigning a haughty expression like a real king. All the kids around them cracked up laughing. Jessica wanted to hurl.

"I won't. I'm not going to dance with him," Jessica shouted. "I'll rescind the crown. The runner-up can have it."

"Oh, no, you won't," Elizabeth said, stepping closer to her. "If you do that I'll tell everyone what you did to Enid. This school can forgive a lot, Jess, but not something that outright cruel and selfish."

Jessica gulped. She had never seen Elizabeth look so mad. Not even when she'd found out how Jessica had tried to steal Todd.

"And I'll do you one better," Elizabeth whispered. "If you don't dance with Win and smile and make it look good for the cameras, *I'll* never forgive you."

There was no air in Jessica's lungs. For the first time since her whole plot began, she felt that she might have stepped over the line. Even if she *had* thought she was doing both Liz and Ronnie a favor. But she couldn't lose her sister. That was not something she was willing to risk.

"Okay, fine," Jessica said finally. "I'll do it. But if you think I'm going to do anything gross like kiss that loser, you're insane."

Elizabeth smiled, as if the idea were just occurring to her. "I like that idea! Winston would be *so* excited. You can be really sweet when you want to be, you know?"

Jessica paled as Winston finally reached her side. "Oh, no. Liz!"

"Sorry, Jess!" Elizabeth said with a shrug, sinking back into the crowd.

Winston held out his hand to Jessica. Behind her, she felt the crowd shift as they cleared a big spot in the center of the basketball court. The spotlight flicked on, humming audibly. Jessica swallowed a huge lump in her throat.

"May I have this dance, my queen?" Winston joked.

Ugh! Was that broccoli in his teeth?

"Whatever," Jessica said.

Behind her, Elizabeth cleared her throat. Oh, right. She was supposed to make this look good, wasn't she?

"I mean, of course . . . Your Majesty," she said, trying not to sneer.

Winston's face completely lit up. He led Jessica to the middle of the floor, somehow managing not to trip either of them in the process. He placed his sweaty hands on her gorgeous dress, and, holding her breath, she draped her arms over his shoulders.

"I've been daydreaming about this moment my entire life," Winston said.

Jessica flinched. Her eyes darted to Bruce, who was horribly front and center for this awful spectacle. "Yeah. Me too," she said flatly.

"And now, the spotlight dance," Mr. Collins said in a smooth, low voice.

The music started up and Jessica and Winston started to dance. All around them, their classmates snapped pictures, and the videographer for the video yearbook circled them like a true documentary filmmaker. Jessica tried to turn her face away from all the lenses, but there were just too many. Wherever she looked, she was looking at a camera.

"Stop there for a sec, you two," the yearbook photographer requested, hoisting his camera.

Winston held Jessica a bit tighter and Jessica grimaced. Then she saw Elizabeth watching and put on a huge, happy smile. The man took his shot, but then Elizabeth whispered something in his ear and smirked.

I'll kill you. I really will kill you, Jessica thought, glowering at Liz.

"That's right! How about a kiss?" the photographer shouted.

Many of the kids laughed, knowing just how ridiculous the idea was, no doubt. But then someone started chanting.

"Kiss! Kiss! Kiss!"

The voice sounded a lot like Todd. Another person to kill. Winston's eyes were wide with anticipation. Jessica felt bile rising up her throat.

"Kiss! Kiss! Kiss!"

More people joined in the chant.

"Kiss! Kiss! Kiss!"

It was fairly deafening now. Winston closed his eyes and puckered up. Jessica held her breath.

I will *get you for this, Elizabeth Wakefield,* she vowed.

Then she closed her eyes and planted a quick peck on

Winston's overly moist lips. Cheers filled the gym, louder than they'd ever been for any basketball game.

"Way to go, Wakefield!" Bruce shouted, clapping loudly.

Jessica wanted to cry. She wanted to turn around and run. But there was no way she was going to humiliate herself that way. Instead, she forced herself to look at Bruce and shoot him a sardonic smile. He nodded to her, and her heart warmed slightly. It was as if they had a mutual understanding. She was only doing this to be nice. They both knew Winston was so beneath her. Maybe there was still hope for her and Bruce after all.

"Thanks, Jess. That was amazing," Winston said, as if she'd just given him the lip-lock to end all lip-locks.

"Yeah, yeah," Jessica said. "You'd better remember it, because there's no more where that came from."

Winston laughed, as if he thought she was kidding, and adjusted his grip on her waist. "Whatever you say, my queen."

Jessica took a deep breath for patience and closed her eyes. If she tried really, really hard, she could almost imagine that she was dancing with Bruce instead of Winston. She imagined Bruce's strong arms in place of Winston's scrawny ones. Held her breath against Winston's halitosis and recalled that yummy scent Bruce had been wearing. In her mind's eye, Bruce's eyes grew heavy as he leaned down to touch his sweet lips to hers. . . .

And then Winston's foot ground down on Jessica's toe.

"Ow!"

Winston sucked air through his teeth. "Sorry."

So much for daydreams.

CHAPTER

1

"Winston, quit trying to hold my hand!" Jessica Wakefield whispered fiercely as she walked up the steps to the Sweet Valley High gym. Inside, the music was already pumping, and through the high windows she could hear hundreds of voices chatting and laughing. Her pulse started to race with excitement, just like it did before any big event. Of course, it would have been racing a lot faster if she'd been walking through the doors of the annual dance competition with the guy she wanted to be there with—Bruce Patman—rather than with the biggest dork in school.

"I wasn't trying to hold your hand," Winston Egbert said, his brown eyes widening behind his thick glasses. "I just tripped and my fingers happened to graze yours. It was totally not on purpose."

Jessica didn't buy it for a second. Winston had been crushing on her since kindergarten and had practically fallen all over himself when they had been elected homecoming king and queen at the dance a few weeks ago. And now here they were, attending the annual Athletic Department fund-raiser together thanks to some stupid, archaic tradition. Jessica could only imagine who had come up with the rule that the king and the queen had to attend school functions as a couple for the entire fall semester. *Probably some evil spinster principal who never knew true love herself and got her jollies out of messing with teenagers' young, hopeful lives,* she thought.

Of course, Jessica wouldn't have minded the rule at all if Bruce had been elected king, but he hadn't. Instead, the cruelest prank of the century had been pulled by Jessica's very own twin sister, Elizabeth, and now Jess was saddled with Winston "Two Left Feet" Egbert for the annual dance competition—a competition she would have won hands down with Bruce, or any other guy in the school, but had little hope of even placing in with Winston as her partner.

"Let's just get this over with," Jessica grumbled, shoving through the door.

"Your wish is my command, milady," Winston said with a bow. Then he really did trip himself as he chased after her.

As soon as Jessica walked into the gym, she was surrounded by a group of friends. She only half listened to their compliments on her slinky green dress and their random bits of gossip while her eyes scanned the room. It took almost no time to pick out Bruce Patman from the crowd. His tall frame, dark hair, and chiseled good looks set him apart from all the scrawny, pimply losers who had yet to make it through puberty. Jessica felt a thrill go right through her just from looking at him. He was wearing a dark blue shirt and black pants and leaning against the wall with some of his friends from the tennis team, totally comfortable in his own skin.

What she wouldn't give to have a confident, sexy date like that instead of—

"Oops!" Winston collided with her. "Watch it, dude. I'm walking here," he said to whomever had knocked him over.

"Winston, get it together," Jessica said through clenched teeth. "If you can't even walk straight, there's no way we're going to make it through the first round."

Winston's cheeks turned pink. "Sorry, Jess. But don't worry. I've been practicing my moves." He did some strange, jolting arm movements that would have been life-threatening had they been standing any closer to one another.

Could this be any worse? Jessica wondered.

"Jessica! Omigod! I love your dress! I just love it!" Robin Wilson screeched, appearing as if from nowhere. She grabbed Jessica's wrists in her chubby hands and flung her arms out, the better to admire Jessica's outfit. "Where did you get it? I must have one!"

Jessica yanked her arms away from Robin's death grip. The girl was new in school and had, for some reason, latched on to Jessica like a big fat barnacle on the bow of a sleek speedboat. Jessica was too polite—in public, anyway—to tell the girl to get a life and leave her alone, so she was forced to endure scenes like this one over and over again.

"Thanks, Robin," Jessica said. "But I think I got the last one, actually."

Her eyes ran over Robin's muumuu-style dress and she tried not to grimace. The girl would not be able to pull off Jessica's outfit after a month on Weight Watchers, but it wasn't as if she could say that to her face. At least Robin had done something with her plain brown hair for once. It was back in a cool-looking updo, which would have been fine if it hadn't had the unfortunate side effect of making her chubby cheeks appear even chubbier.

"Listen, I have to talk to Lila before the competition starts," Jessica said. "I'll catch up with you later."

"Okay! Yeah! Later!" Robin called after her.

Jessica's best friend, Lila Fowler, was standing in a klatch of people near the refreshment table, wearing a trendy yellow dress that had been ripped right from the pages of *In Style* magazine. She smoothed her light brown hair as Jessica approached.

"*What* was *that*?" she sneered in Robin's direction.

"Oh, just my *biggest* fan," Jessica joked. "Why doesn't she just leave me alone already? If she would give up the stalking, she'd have more time to exercise."

"Jess, you are so bad," Lila said with a smirk.

Jessica shrugged. "It's a gift."

Onstage, Valley of Death, the only student band even remotely worth listening to, finished up their set. Mr. Collins, English teacher and—in Jessica's opinion—major hottie, bounded onto the stage and grabbed the microphone.

"Good evening, ladies and gentlemen!" he intoned in a radio-DJ voice.

"Good evening, Mr. Collins!" the crowd singsonged back in unison, affectionately mocking his master-of-ceremonies act.

"Welcome to Sweet Valley High's twentieth annual dance competition!" he called out.

Everyone cheered like mad. Five years ago, when Jessica's brother had been at SVH, the students—at least, the cooler students—had avoided this fund-raiser. But since all the crazy reality-TV dance competitions had started popping up, it had become one of the most popular events of the year.

"You know the rules. The band will play for an hour," Mr. Collins explained. "While our contestants dance, the judges will circulate about the floor, checking out your technique, your originality, and your overall performance. Then, after a short break so they can tally their scores, the winners will be announced."

"Oh my God. Let's get on with it already!" Jessica said through her teeth.

"Everybody ready?" he asked.

"Yes!" everyone shouted.

"Then let's get started! It's SVH tradition that we lead off the competition with our homecoming king and queen. Jessica Wakefield and Winston Egbert, would you please take the center of the floor?"

Jessica cringed as everyone clapped. "Have fun!" Lila said, teasing her and slapping her on the back. Jessica shot her a look of death as she walked to the center of the dance floor, meeting Winston under the spotlight.

"And away we go!" Mr. Collins shouted.

Behind the drum set, Emily Mayer counted out a beat. "One! Two! One, two, three, four!"

"Do not screw this up for me, Winston," Jessica said under her breath.

"Don't worry, Jess. I'm on it," Winston replied.

And then he launched into the most ridiculous combination of dance moves Jessica had ever seen. It was like early Michael Jackson meets old man attempting to swing dance meets boy choking on his own saliva. Everyone around the dance floor started to laugh, so Jessica did the only thing she could think of. She started dancing on her own, pretending Winston wasn't even there.

Soon the rest of the dancers had joined them on the floor, and Jessica imagined she was dancing with the cute sophomore behind her rather than with Winston Egbert. That worked for a while, until Winston's foot came down squarely on top of her own, for the third time.

"Winston! What are you trying to do? Put me in the hospital?" she hissed, clutching her foot.

"I'm so sorry, Jess," he said, going white as a sheet. "I didn't mean to . . ."

But Jessica didn't hear a word he was saying, because walking up behind him, like a white knight in a fairy tale, was Bruce Patman himself. He smiled in a conspiratorial way at Jessica, as if they were sharing some private joke, and tapped Winston on the shoulder.

"I think your work here is finished, Egbert," he said, in that low sexy voice of his. "Watch how it's done."

Then he took Jessica's hand, pulled her to him, and started to dance. Jessica could hardly breathe. She was in Bruce Patman's arms. He'd saved her right there in front of the entire school. And wow, could this guy ever dance.

"Better?" he asked, an amused glint in his eyes as he looked down at her.

Jessica tipped her head back and smiled, her heart pounding erratically. "Much."

• • •

"Okay, what just happened?" Elizabeth Wakefield asked Todd Wilkins as they stood in the bleachers. All around them, couples were making their way to the dance floor to join Jessica and Bruce while Winston stood by looking like a dejected puppy.

"I'd say Her Highness just struck again," Todd replied, taking Elizabeth's hand. Together they navigated the bleachers until they hit the freshly polished basketball court. "Not that I'm surprised. Jessica always gets what she wants, no matter who she has to obliterate in the process."

"Todd!" Elizabeth scolded, even though she knew he was telling the truth.

"Liz!" he mimicked in reply, giving her a teasing smile.

Elizabeth couldn't help smiling back as he led her to the dance floor. In fact, most of her time with Todd was spent smiling uncontrollably. They had already been going out for a few weeks, but sometimes Elizabeth still couldn't believe that the guy of her dreams was now her boyfriend. Every time she looked into Todd's warm brown eyes, she practically melted. And she knew that her sister felt the same way about Bruce Patman. Liz also knew she should be happy for Jessica for finally snagging a dance with the boy she'd been in love with half her life. And she would have been—if the object of her sister's affection had been anyone other than that arrogant, self-centered serial dater Bruce Patman. Of course, Bruce had always pretty much ignored Jessica, so Elizabeth had never had to worry about him before. But now, as Valley of Death switched to a slow song, Bruce was pulling Jessica to him and holding on to her so tightly they could have been one person. It looked like he'd finally woken up and smelled the beauty.

"What brought this on?" Elizabeth mused as Todd moved back and forth to the lilting beat. "Why has Bruce suddenly noticed Jessica now?"

"Knowing him, he probably just wants to win the contest and he realized Jessica was the best partner for the job," Todd said, theorizing.

Sure enough, an hour later, when Mr. Collins announced the winners, no one was surprised by the results.

"And this year's Sweet Valley High dance champions are . . . Jessica Wakefield and Bruce Patman!" he exclaimed. Jessica squealed happily and jumped into Bruce's arms. Bruce squeezed her so tightly it made Elizabeth squirm from halfway across the room. "And now you two can lead us in the next dance," Mr. Collins told them.

As Jessica and Bruce moved together once more, Elizabeth spotted Winston drowing his sorrows in root beer by the refreshment table.

"Look at Winston," she said, nudging her boyfriend. "I feel so bad for him."

"Come on. We'll go cheer him up," Todd suggested.

Walking hand in hand, Elizabeth and Todd joined Winston near the wall.

"For a guy who's usually in the middle of everything, you're pretty quiet tonight," Elizabeth remarked.

Winston smiled broadly, but it was clearly forced. "Just taking a time-out. We homecoming kings have a lot of responsibilities."

"Don't let Jessica get to you, Win," Liz said. "She's very 'act now, think later,' if you know what I mean."

"Whatever. I get it. She doesn't want to dance with someone who could maim her beyond repair," he said with a shrug. "So she danced with Bruce. She's still going to Ken's after-party with me."

"You sure about that?" Todd asked, taking a slug of soda.

"Don't worry about me, guys. I can handle Jessica Wakefield," Winston said.

Todd shot him a dubious look and Elizabeth felt sorry for the guy. It was amazing to her that after worshipping Jessica from afar for so many years, he seemed to know so little about her. But then, love was blind, right?

Valley of Death finished their last song and the lights flicked on, effectively ending the dance portion of the evening. Instantly, the band members congregated around the refreshment table, snagging drinks and snacks after a hard night's work. Emily Mayer, Elizabeth's and Todd's friend and the drummer in the band, came right over to them, starry-eyed. Her dark hair was combed into her face, and her eyes were rimmed with kohl black liner.

She was wearing a faded black T-shirt with a red peace sign on the front and baggy shorts with combat boots.

"You guys are never going to believe this!" she said, her skin glistening with sweat. "We just got a manager!"

"What? No way!" Elizabeth exclaimed.

"Yep! See that guy talking to Dana?" She pointed out the group's lead singer, who was near the back entrance of the gym, her head bent as she listened to a guy in a black suit and sunglasses. Sunglasses at night, indoors. "He saw the video Guy posted on YouTube and came to check us out. He wants to sign us!"

"Emily, that's unbelievable," Todd said. "Congratulations!"

"Are you sure he's a real manager?" Elizabeth asked.

"Liz! Burst her bubble, why don't you?" Todd scolded her.

"Sorry. Guess it's just the reporter in me," Elizabeth said sheepishly.

"Please. It's a totally legitimate question. His name's Tony Conover and he works for T. G. Goode in L.A.," Emily explained, pushing her dark hair over her shoulder. "They're this huge agency that's worked with August Moon and Savage. His specialty is scouring the web for new talent. He wants to book us some gigs and see how we do on a larger stage. I'm so psyched, you guys! This could really be it! Valley of Death! Opening for Coldplay!"

"Unbelievable, Em! I'm so happy for you!" Elizabeth said, giving her friend a hug.

"You so have to do an article about this for The Oracle," Emily trilled.

"Definitely," Elizabeth replied.

"Well, Dana's flagging us down. I'd better go. Don't want my new manager to think I'm not focused!" Emily said. "See you guys later!"

"Yeah! If you don't forget about the little people!" Todd called after her.

Elizabeth sighed as the band gathered around Tony Conover, enraptured by every word he said. Kind of the same way Jessica had been acting with Bruce all night. Liz glanced around for her sister as the dance started to break up. She found Jessica on the other side of the room, talking intently with Winston, who looked none too pleased.

"Looks like someone's already blowing off the little people," she said under her breath. She gave Todd a quick kiss. "I'll be right back."

There was a certain twin sister she had to set straight.